River of Murder

Conrad Jestmore

Copyright 2012 by Conrad Jestmore

All rights reserved

This is a work of fiction. As such, all characters in it do not exist in real life. Names, characters and incidents are products of the author's imagination.

*****

Dead on the river, like a floating swan,
Oh, the wind and the rain.
Traditional Ballad

To Donna, with love, who demanded perseverance.

ALSO BY CONRAD JESTMORE

Kodak Black and White (Memoir)

Goonybirds (Memoir)

A Roadmap to Hope (Poetry)

A Christmas Carol: A Spirited New Musical (Play)

1

When the corpse on the table is a friend, it's hard to be objective. It wasn't the first time someone I loved was laid out before me, but it was still difficult. Vernon Johnson was on the mortuary table in front of me. He was my life-long friend, and I loved the man dearly.

Vernon Johnson. Aged seventy-nine. Left side of face obliterated, as if a candle melted and someone scraped away the tallow. Torso crushed and chest caved in. Ligature marks to the neck. Livor mortis coloration on abdomen, thighs and chest. So much for objectivity.

Vernon Johnson. Old man Johnson. Taught me a two-seam fastball. Might have married my mother if his best friend, my dad, hadn't stolen her away from him. Didn't say anything when his son Bob and I used to go cat-fishing on the Little Arkansas when Bob should have been doing his farm chores. Got red in the face from yelling at us when he found plugs of Skoal in our jeans' pockets. Stood up for me at my wedding and comforted me when my wife died. Now, there's some objectivity for you.

He was the last of Bob's and my parents to go, and it was a shame to see him like this. It tore my heart up.

"I need to use your phone, Sam." Sam Watson, our local mortician, walked in the embalming room from an adjoining work room. He's short and thin and he looked up at me through a pair of pince-nez glasses that gave him a sort of reptilian look.

"Use the one on the wall there, Jimmy." He was in his work apron and he wiped his hands on a towel and walked out again. I had lied to him in order to see Vernon's body and told him I was working for the family. In fact, I told Bob I wouldn't take the case, not just because I don't do that sort of work anymore, but because it didn't seem from what he told me on the phone there even was a case. It was just a typical farm accident involving a tractor. Tractors are notorious for those kinds of things, especially the old ones.

I dialed Bob Johnson's home number on the old rotary phone. The weight of the dial against my fingers was something I hadn't felt in a long time and it felt good.

"Bob? Jimmy O'Reilly. I need to ask you a few questions, if that's okay."

"Sure." He was grieving and his voice seemed far away.

"I'm sorry I doubted you when you said you suspected foul play in your father's death. I've taken a look at Vernon's remains and I want you to authorize a body transfer to the coroner for an autopsy."

"I don't want no autopsy," Bob said, which was a typical response I was used to hearing from family members. "I don't want nobody to cut Dad open."

"I understand your concern." I hesitated for a moment, pulled my lapis stone turtle from my pocket, flipped it in the air and took the plunge. "If you want me to investigate, you'll need to ask for an autopsy."

"You mean you'll take the case?"

All my instincts cautioned me against it. I had a nice, quiet skip trace practice going for me. Although I maintained my P.I. license, I'd left the violence and confusion of police and private investigative work behind me and didn't miss it one bit.

"Yeah," I said. "I'll take it. I'm going to put Sam on. Give your approval so he can make arrangements to transfer Vernon's body.

I had to get out of the frigid air conditioning that shut my senses down, so I walked through the show room of caskets, past the front desk sign that read "Full Service Graveside Planning. Pricing Options Available," and out onto the blacktop parking lot and the heat and humidity of a June Kansas day. A minute later, Sam came out, the towel draped over one shoulder.

"Sam, why did Phil tell you not to let anybody but family view Vernon's body?"

"I couldn't say, Jimmy? Those were his instructions."

Phil was the local deputy handling the case and, among other things, Bob told me it had been filed as accidental.

"Who signed for cause on the death certificate for Vernon?"

"Phil had Doc Smally come over for that."

"Why? He wouldn't be in his office on Sunday, and one of the itinerant doctors would have been on duty up the street at the clinic."

"Maybe Phil thought it would be better to stick with the family doctor. I don't know."

"Besides, Doc couldn't sign off on an accidental death, you know that. A coroner has to sign. The State won't accept it that way."

"After he talked with Phil, Doc changed it, called it a natural death. Said it was cardiac arrest. He'd been treating him for hypertension for a couple of years and I guess he figured he'd had a heart attack, lost control and the tractor rolled over on him."

"You comfortable with that, considering the ligature marks on the neck?"

"It's not my place to raise those issues. I'm just doing my job."

"Which coroner is going to get it?" I asked.

"I'll send him into Wichita." He walked back inside to the frigid air leaving me sweating on the blacktop.

Phil Turffe was one of our local three-member police department in Chisholm who came to us three years ago from some small town in eastern Colorado. He was short and round with absolutely no sense of humor. Locals nicknamed him Phil Dirt, but his mean-spirited nature caused them to drop it quickly. He was a real asshole. I didn't know what he was up to, but if he was switching cause of death around to suit his needs and ignoring obvious signs of possible foul play, then he wasn't only an asshole, he was dirty, to boot. I wasn't about to let it slide.

It was time to get in Phil's face.

2

Phil's short fat body came running toward me.
"Go back Jimmy, go back. Get outta here." His pudgy arms thrashed over his head as he yelled at me to turn around and his protruding neck swiveled back and forth as he ran. He looked like my pet turtle, Tiresias, when he'd get flipped over and try to right himself.

When I reached him at the side of Johnson's north field, his face puffed and flushed red and sweat trickled down his cheeks. Little blue veins threaded his jowls.

I started soft by putting on my silly Irish grin that convinced people I was friendly and harmless when I wanted them to think that. "I've just come out to look around a little, Phil."

"Can't do it. We got the place taped off." He was still yelling even though we were face to face now.

"I noticed. The yellow tape was hard to miss when I had to step over it to cross the drive. What's up with that?"

"Just a precaution."

"I thought Vernon's death was accidental. You find evidence of a crime?" I kept an innocent tone and didn't let on I knew there'd been a change in how the death was filed.

"No. Nothing like that. Not at all. We just want to make sure we haven't missed anything."

This made no sense at all in light of either an accidental or natural-cause death, but again, I said nothing, just smiling and nodding my head, and then walked right passed him to Vernon's over-turned tractor. It was an old, red 1960s Massey Ferguson, and lay on its side at the bottom of a swale, its needle-nose pointing, like the hands of a compass, off toward the Little Arkansas River just on the other side of the swale's crest. There was mud caked on the wheels from an area that hadn't dried out from the last rain.

"Is this how Vernon died?"

"He was under the nose, face up, life crushed outta him. One of those classic farm accidents. Tragic and entirely preventable. These things should never happen. But you got to leave now, Jimmy, and I'm not fooling."

I ignored the command. "Who all's been out here, Phil?"

"Bob found him, and then me and the two paramedics that took him in, but you-"

"Then what are those footprints over there?" I walked past the tractor where there were other prints, and not the same size or kind that led to and from the tractor. This time he ignored my question.

"Okay for you, Jimmy, I'm calling for back-up." He pulled a two-way out of his belt."

"Back-up to handle me? That surprises me, Phil." I flashed my Irish grin as I grabbed his free arm to get purchase and pull myself up the slick side of the swale. He flinched in surprise at the physical contact. "You ought to be able to handle an old fart like me." I walked past him, heading back across the field and toward the farmhouse.

"Oh." I turned back. "One other thing. What was Vernon doing out here on a Sunday morning?"

"I don't know. Maybe Bob knows the answer to that one."

I dropped my grin and started back toward him, more aggressive now. "You didn't ask? Not very thorough for someone who's trying to make sure he doesn't miss anything. Say, why'd you go get Doc Smally when a clinic doctor would have been on duty?" I kept hammering away at him.

"Well-" He stammered for an answer. "It... it just seemed the right thing to do."

"By the way, you looking for bones?"

"What the hell you talking about, Jimmy?"

"Bob told me Vernon found bones out here, down on the river, and he told me he told you about it." I stepped up close and got in his face, and he staggered back a step, his two-way dropping onto the caked mud at the edge of the swale, static spewing forth.

"What if? There's all kinds of critters dragging bones to and from the Arkan-saw."

"You been here three years Phil, and you still don't get it. We call it the Our-Kansas here, not the Arkan-saw. Get with the program or move on further east."

I turned and left both him and his two-way sputtering in the afternoon heat.

3

I parked my pickup about a quarter of a mile down the county dirt road over a culvert and behind some Osage trees and thick brush where I could neither be seen nor see anything myself, and cut the engine. It was hot and muggy, even in the shade, and with my windows down, bottle flies kept buzzing in and out of the cab. That was the only sound, and in the silence it was easy to hear Phil's engine when he started up his patrol car back at the Johnson place. I had waited less than a half an hour, and now, two minutes later he came down the road on the other side of the Osage trees, a thick plume of road dust scouring up behind him. Some of it filtered through the tree leaves and settled in around me.

I waited another five minutes until he was well back onto the two-lane heading into town, then started my engine and drove back to the farm. Like all the others in this area, it sits in the Arkansas River Lowlands, rich soil between and along the Big and Little Arkansas Rivers a bit north and west of Wichita, where the rivers finally come together at the confluence.

I must have spent close to an hour nosing around the place, not entirely sure what I was looking for, a skeleton, a pile of bones, a skull, a single leg or arm bone. Maybe something that didn't even exist. Bob just said bones when he told me on the phone what had happened, and I discounted it at the time as the mental ramblings of someone early in the grieving process.

I wandered through the house, one of those late 1800s jobs, two story, built solid, and like most of them still standing, very functional. I wriggled my body through an opening in the limestone blocks and looked in the crawl space under the house, inspected the barn and other out-buildings, lifted the door to the storm cellar and went down in it, and looked down a well casing. Nothing.

Then I noticed Vernon's car. It sat next to the pole barn at an angle, which was curious, because Vernon was meticulous about his vehicles. He always put the car inside the pole barn. I opened one door and inspected the interior of the maroon Mercury two-door. It was clean. Vacuumed. Nothing out of place. Not a speck of dust or crumpled paper anywhere. The glove compartment had a tire pressure gauge and an owner's manual. There was a vanity mirror behind the passenger's visor, but when I lowered the driver's visor, there was a piece of paper folded neatly and stuck in an attached clip. I opened it and saw precisely drawn lines made with a pencil and one squiggly line off toward the edge that slanted and intersected some of the straight lines and then a single dot in the middle of it all, and on the back was one penciled word: blondie. I turned it back over and looked at the lines again. They looked like a graphing exercise from a high school math class.

I refolded the paper, put it in my shirt pocket, and then got out to look at the tires. They, like the car itself, were fairly new, and the tread was deep. The back tires had some gravel imbedded in them but were otherwise clean. But the front tires had a black substance caked in the tread, like dried mud. When I pried a piece out and brought it up close for inspection, it had an intense, sour smell to it, that seemed familiar in a way, yet I couldn't put my finger on what it was. It was almost like sewer gas in solid form. I put the piece in a small envelope and pocketed it.

On my way home I thought about why Vernon might have chosen not to park in the pole barn. Or what might have prevented him.

4

My front door was wide open. That meant one of two possibilities. Either an intruder had broken in, or Janie was there. I opted to believe the latter. I paid her to come over two or three times a week, depending on the weather, to water my plants, but she also straightened up, kept track of my refrigerator and left me notes on what I was low on. She was an eighth grader at Chisholm middle school. Her father left when she was two, and her mother was at home, occasionally, depending on whom she might be bedding at any given time, so I figured the odd money and the work might help to keep Janie out of trouble. As it turned out, she kept me out of trouble. She was indispensable. I could see Janie through my French doors out on the terrace holding a watering can over a rosemary shrub.

"Janie, you can use the hose, it's quicker than refilling the watering can." I tell her that every time she comes over, but she always prefers the can.

"Oh, hello Mr. O'Reilly. That's okay, I don't mind."

I've also told her to call me Jimmy or just plain O'Reilly, without the mister, but that never took either and I've given up on that one.

"I'm just finishing up with your herbs, Mr. O'Reilly. The basil was a might parched, so you better keep an eye on it."

To my mind, she sounded like a thirty year old in the skinny, awkward body of an eighth grader.

"Also, I fed Ty some watermelon rinds, but you'd better watch out for him. He's blind as a bat, and I think he might have trampled a couple of basil stems. Ever since you took his pen down, he's been on a rampage."

When Tiresias had shown up on my front porch two years ago, his shell was cracked, probably from being clipped by a car, a wandering Ornate Box Turtle who came in off the road, choosing my porch for shelter and safety. I didn't even know he was blind for three months until I took him to a vet because I thought he had parasites. When I found out he couldn't see, I changed his name from Boxie to Tiresias after the blind Greek fortune teller.

Anyway, I duct taped his cracked shell shut and kept him in a wire pen next to the terrace until it healed. Now he roamed free, having memorized every rock and obstacle in my back yard.

"I have a couple of questions," Janie said, as she set down the galvanized can and walked back inside with me following. Janie has dark hair that frames her oval face, and she often affects an intense look while she squints, even when she's just asking a casual question, like she did then. "Did you want this book of poems you left open re-shelved, or should I just leave it out? I know you're particular about your books."

She was referring to the volume of Yeats I had been reading. "Go ahead and leave it there," I said. "That is an on-going project." I found myself squinting back at her, involuntarily.

"Okay. You know, I read a few of those poems and they're all about death."

"Those are mostly from late in his life when he knew his time was near, so he was thinking about it a lot." I don't know why I was attempting to justify Yeats' poems to a thirteen year-old.

"There's one about dancing days in there. I thought that would be happy, but it's all about dead children and really gross things."

"True, but do you remember the refrain? 'I carry the sun in a golden cup, and the moon in a silver bag.'"

She squinted as she thought for a moment. "That's impossible. Nobody can do that."

"Not literally, but it is a nice thought, don't you think?"

She thought for another moment, then said, "It seems like a heavy burden to me. Anyway, I think a poem about dancing ought to be happy."

"You do have a point, Janie." Although I was thinking more about the heavy burden part than the happy part.

She squinted at me for a moment and then said, "You seem a little down, Mr. O'Reilly. Is anything wrong?"

How do you tell a thirteen year-old who has been reading poems about death that someone in the community has just died?

"I found out that a good friend of mine has passed away, Janie."

Her squinty eyes suddenly got wide. "Who's that?"

"Vernon Johnson."

"You mean the hardware store owner's father? That old man who lives out east of town?"

"That's him. Bob Johnson's father. He was a close friend of my parents when they were living, and a good friend to me my whole life."

"Gee, I'm sorry. I guess all that stuff about death in those poems wasn't a good thing for me to bring up."

"It's okay, Janie. You didn't know."

"Well, if there's anything I can do, you let me know." She stared down at the floor.

"Thank you. You'd just best get on home. Your mom will be wondering."

"She hasn't been around for a couple of days. Oh, by the way," she said, "You're low on olive oil. You may want to order another case from that place in Italy you get it from. What's it called?"

"Tuscany. You're the best, Janie. Thanks."

"And, oh, when I dusted your turtle collection I noticed the blue one's gone, but you have a new little fellow in there with the others."

I looked over at my stone figures on top of the bookshelf. "The red one? I picked him up last week. He's Red Jasper."

"Whatever."

"That's for strength and endurance."

"Cool. Well, he's pretty. I like him. I'll see you later in the week, depending on whether it rains or no." She was out the front door, her flip-flops clomping with her awkward steps. I was never quite sure whether I was a father figure to her, or if she was a mother figure to me.

I picked up the red turtle and admired its smooth, mottled surface. My collection had been mere set decoration and sat idle for far too long. The previous week I decided it was time I started using it again and had slipped the blue one in my pocket. I knew Ty would approve. I could feel its protective stone of hard lapis against my thigh as I picked up the Yeats volume and walked back out on the terrace.

My bungalow sat on the west edge of Chisholm, and from my terrace I looked out over a wheat field and sat rereading "Those Dancing Days Are Gone." I had always thought of the sun and moon images as glorious, never as a burden, but maybe Janie had something there.

I looked up at the field of gold. The wheat was at that in-between stage. Those early hues of rust had been left behind and now it had that bright gold intensity it gets just before going to that dull, flat color of ripened wheat, and the custom cutters come roaring through on their combines. A dull, flat color like hammered gilt. The color of my wife's hair when she was still alive.

Tiresias, my blind rescue turtle, emerged from a sage bush, ambled his shoebox sized body across the flagstones and stopped in front of me.

"Good afternoon, Ty," I said.

He looked up, his cloudy eyes nodding a sightless greeting. Ty always looked at me as if he knew something I didn't, and as if he wanted to tell me something about it. I almost always half-expected him to. Then he wandered off and disappeared into the basil.

A golden cup of sun, a silver bag of moon, a blind turtle and a blue lapis stone. I figured it was time to start asking questions.

5

"The last time I saw Dad alive?"

Bob sat on his front porch step answering my questions. All I knew so far was what he had told me on the phone when he first called and then what I saw at Watson's Funeral home when I viewed Vernon's remains. I figured I needed to ask Bob some hard questions.

"That was yesterday morning in Latte Dottie's when we ate breakfast."

Latte Dottie's is Chisholm's coffee shop and diner on the main drag, Commercial Street.

"Let me take that back," he said. "It was outside Dottie's. We stood talking and chewing on toothpicks after breakfast, and then he got in his Mercury when I walked off to open the hardware store."

"Which way did he drive off?"

"Don't know. I mean, I had no reason to notice."

"And neither you or LaVonda or anybody else you know of heard from him or saw him again until you found him this morning under his tractor?"

"Nobody."

"What was he wearing at Dottie's?"

"He had that green leisure suit on of his. But why is that important?"

"Was that what he had on when you found him?"

"Come to think of it, it was, and that's kind of funny, 'cause he knows I always come to pick him up for church Sunday morning. He wouldn't be dressed in that. See, none of this makes any sense to me. He had no reason to be out there in the field in the first place, and even if he was, he's too good of a farmer to make a mistake like that, I don't care what the conditions of that field were. I don't know that I would've even gone out there to look for him, but old Tick here, he was whining and circling and begging me to follow him."

Vernon's blue hound, Tick, lay curled next to Bob.

'I thought about Bob's parents, Vernon and Emily, and how they'd been such close friends with my parents. After my father stole Vernon's girl away from him, and when the two men returned from the war, the four of them double-dated in my father's old '37 Plymouth coupe. I'd seen black and white photos of the four of them leaning against the side of the coupe, the men in their felt fedoras and the women in their long, print cotton dresses.

"You and I go back a long way, Bob, our parents being so close and all, and you and me wandering your fields when we were kids. And high school baseball."

"Yeah, I'll never forget State. You pitching the championship game and me catching."

I looked at his tall, lean body hunched over on the steps, his black hair slicked straight back and his big, hooked nose. He was a carbon copy of Vernon at that age.

"It's just, I don't want you getting the wrong idea, Bob. I'm asking you some hard questions at a rough time."

"I know. It's something you got to do."

"Who would want to see Vernon dead?"

"Ain't nobody I can think of. Everybody loved Dad. He'd go out of his way to help a stranger."

"I know that, but think. Anybody at all that might have had a grievance, or maybe held an old grudge of some kind against your dad."

"Well, there was that deal with Buford."

"Buford Thomas?" I said. He'd bought the place north of Vernon's a couple of years ago at auction.

"Sure. Dad and him had a difference of opinion awhile back. They got into it over water. Buford didn't get any water rights when he bought that place, so he'd been siphoning surface water off the river to irrigate his corn. Dad found fish kills from the low water level, and I guess, from what he told me, him and Buford went at it a few times. Some pretty harsh words was said."

"Doesn't seem like something you'd kill a man over."

"No, but Buford, he's got himself a temper. Hard telling what he might do with someone getting under his skin like that."

"Tell me more about these bones you claim he saw. Did you actually see them?"

"I never saw 'em. All I know is he said he found bones down next to the river where it cuts across the northeast side of our property, and they was human. He was certain of that. He kept thinking and talking about 'em. He seemed obsessed by them. Fact is, that's what he kept going on about while we was eating breakfast at Dottie's."

LaVonda came out on the porch and handed us each a glass of iced tea.

"Thank you LaVonda. I'm sorry for your troubles, and I'm sorry to be intruding at a time like this."

"That's alright, Jimmy. We're just thankful you're willing to help out." I could see the redness around her eyes from her crying, and she fought back tears as she carried out her hostess duties, even as she grieved. She excused herself and went back inside.

"Why do you think Vernon parked his car outside the pole barn?"

"That don't make no sense neither, Jimmy. I just don't know."

I took out the sheet of paper I'd found behind the visor. "You ever see this? Do you know what it is?" I turned it over so he could see both sides.

"No. Just looks like a bunch of scribbling to me. And blondie? He quit reading the comics years ago. Said he thought times had changed and the funny paper wasn't funny no more."

"How about this?" I held the piece of caked mud from the Mercury's tire under his nose and he flinched.

"Whew. Howdy. That stinks. I ain't smelled that in years."

"Then you recognize it?"

"Sure. Don't you? Remember when we kept those pigs for awhile on the farm? That spot stunk for years after we got rid of them."

Then it came back to me. The intense smell of a pig sty. "Where would Vernon have been recently that has pigs?"

"Nowheres I can think of. But what does that have to do with anything?"

"Just some possible leads. Bob, I want you to keep me up to date on anything Phil says to you or asks you to do. Would you do that for me?"

"Sure, if you think it's important."

It was twilight when I left, and I opted to fix myself something quick to eat rather than stopping for a bite. Chisholm is a small town in central Kansas and it only takes a few minutes to drive from one side of town to the other. I drove up Commercial through the main five-block business hub, past the town square with its water tower and the Dairy Queen on the far side of it. I passed Johnson's hardware store, Dottie's coffee shop and the police station. It was a calm, quiet night, and the June heat of the day had started to dissipate. A few lights started to come on here and there, and with the evening serenity, it was difficult to believe, even with my prior experiences in the criminal world, that anyone could have had a reason to commit a violent act upon the man I had known as Vernon Johnson.

I felt the drain of what a long day it had been. It was late, and I hadn't eaten, so it needed to be something quick and simple. In ten minutes I had the pasta ready, al dente, tossed it in my best olive oil, added some chopped tomatoes and black olives, and crumbled feta over the top to melt into it. I grabbed a little basil from the terrace herbs, did a chiffonade, sprinkled it over the top and settled in with a glass of red. Wouldn't you know it, the only thing open was a bottle of Brunello left over from a dinner the previous week. Damn. Sometimes you just have to make do.

While I sipped the Brunello, I kept picturing Bob and Vernon chewing on their toothpicks outside of Dottie's. Someone who was there on Saturday morning surely saw Vernon leave. Someone must know where he went and what he did and how he spent his last few hours. One of those someone's might be Buford Thomas.

6

"I'll have a latte, but with a touch more froth and a little less steamed milk." I said it as seriously as I could, deadpan, as I sat at the counter in Latte Dottie's.

Dottie stared back at me with her steal gray eyes, gave a guttural choke that was her version of a laugh, and walked back into the kitchen.

"Okay. Java, black," I said, knowing I had tempted the Fates and shouldn't go any farther.

Dottie had named her place Latte Dottie's as a joke, because all she served was percolator coffee. Black. In fact, if an uninitiated customer even so much as requested cream or sugar, neither of which would be found on the tables, she would bring out the black coffee in a ceramic mug, bang it down on the surface, and then nod to a small counter mounted on a side wall, her only concession to the changing times. Anyone wanting cream or sugar has to walk over and get his own.

She walked back out from the kitchen and put a mug of black liquid in front of me. "Don't ever say anything like that to me again and expect to get served in here in your lifetime."

"I love you, too." Then, before she could turn, "I heard tell Vernon Johnson had his last meal in here Saturday morning." Dottie's was the hub of morning activity in Chisholm and I figured she, being notorious for her gossip mongering, would know something if anybody did.

"Don't know if it was or not. But he was here, along with Bob. It's terrible, Vernon's passing. You think they'll bury him in one of those places like Arlington, him being a war hero and all?"

Vernon had been heavily decorated as a pilot in World War II. In the last few months of the war in 1945 he flew a DC-3 transport in the South Pacific and his actions were credited with saving the lives of twenty-four other pilots, his cargo, when his plane went down in the Solomon Sea off of New Guinea. He had also been wounded by enemy fire in another incident.

"I doubt that, Dottie. It's probably going to be a small family ceremony out at the cemetery."

"I hear you're investigating this as a crime. Did somebody murder Vernon?"

"Word sure gets around fast in Chisholm."

"Well, a body has a right to wonder and we'd all like to know some details. Did somebody shoot him?"

"It'll all come out eventually, Dottie, just be patient. You notice anything Saturday morning? Anything different when Bob and Vernon were here?"

"So you are investigating. Who do you think did it?"

"Just answer my questions, Dottie. Was there anything peculiar about the way Vernon acted, or anything he did different?"

"No. They both had their usual, paid their check and left."

"Was Buford Thomas here then?"

"No, he wasn't. But Terry and JoAnn was in here then. You might ask them." She nodded to the booth behind me where Terry and JoAnn Billings sat along with their seven year old son Ter Junior.

I swiveled around on my stool and Dottie came around from behind the counter, standing next to us to get a better earful. The Monday morning breakfast crowd had thinned, and the Billings were the only ones left in the diner.

"Couldn't help overhearing, Jimmy. Who murdered Vernon?" Terry was a big burly man, a redhead like me, and he sold little packets of seeds in the seed and feed store.

"We don't know that anybody did, Terry. But did you or JoAnn notice anything Saturday?"

"Not a whit. Everything was A-Okay. Nothing out of kilter that I saw. Both Vernon and Bob looked fit as a fiddle."

"JoAnn? How about you?"

"I didn't see anything." Chisholm's females are often curt in the presence of their spouses.

"I did, Mr. O'Reilly. I noticed something."

I looked over at Ter Junior sitting next to his mom. He's a skinny kid with mop-red hair and ugly as sin.

"You did not." JoAnn hit him on his thigh.

"Did too."

I've always had more faith in the powers of observation of animals and children than I have in adults. Of course the problem is, animals can't talk, and kids are often corrected by grown-ups. If we listen close enough though, the truth is usually there to be found in both cases.

"What did you see?" I asked him.

His buck teeth worked his lower lip over a good one. "I seen him get mad at Billy Jacobs."

"You saw no such of a thing." JoAnn hit his thigh again.

"Did too. I watched him through the window when we was sitting in the booth there in the corner and Billy was kicking a soccer ball over in the square and he ran after his ball when it went in the street and Mr. Johnson stopped his car and got out and yelled at him. He even shook his finger at him."

Terry and JoAnn stared at Ter Junior like he was some kind of alien.

"Did you see anything else?"

"He got back in his car but he didn't go right away. He took something down from that thing in the car that blocks the sun and he looked at it for a while and then put it back."

"Which way did he drive off?" I asked.

"That way." Ter Junior pointed north up Commercial.

When I got up to leave, Dottie gave what passed as a smile for her. It was her gossipy smile of satisfaction and a job well done. Terry and JoAnn both looked sullen, as if they were afraid they had begotten some form of a cretin for their offspring.

Outside I contemplated the implications of what a truth-revealing child had just told me. The graphing exercise and blondie paper behind the visor obviously had importance for Vernon. And why would he drive north? Anything in town is within walking distance, and if he was going to go home he would head south and then east. North of Chisholm is nothing but wheat fields. What was there that could have held interest for him?

I walked up Commercial and climbed the narrow wooden steps to the old second story office Doc Smally had kept for thirty-some years. Jason Bates stood in the hall outside, next to the frosted glass on the door, stenciled in black, block letters that read Doctor Joseph Smally, Family Practice.

Jason, wearing his work clothes from the farm, stood with his hat in his hands and looked puzzled.

"What's the matter, Jason?" I asked.

"This don't make no sense. I had an appointment with Doc this morning, but his door is locked and there's a sign here says he's not here."

I looked, and taped next to the door was a hand-scrawled note that read "Left town. Family emergency."

"Everybody knows, he don't got no more family. He's the only one left," Jason said. "Where could he be?"

"It does seem strange. If it's something you need taking care of right away, maybe you should go to the clinic."

"No, that's okay," he said. "I'll wait till he gets back." He fitted his green John Deere cap on his head and walked back down the stairs.

7

Buford Thomas' place abutted Vernon's on the north, but you couldn't get to it from the Johnson's farm because the county road ended there. You had to go north out of town first and then cut over on a different county road. If the Billing's kid was right about Vernon driving north up Commercial, maybe that's where he was headed.

    I pulled into Buford's rutted drive, past two signs that said No Trespassing and Trespassers Will Be Shot. I immediately noticed what two years of neglect had done to a once well-maintained farm house. The single story structure was nearly bare of paint, some windows were broken out with cardboard duct-taped to the holes, and the guttering and roof were in complete shambles. No vegetation existed anywhere in the yard. A single old pickup of the 1980s variety, a dull, faded black color, sat in the dirt drive, and there were couplings and pipes for an irrigation system stacked off to one side.

I'd never met the man, but I'd heard of how he came here two years ago from Missouri after finding the property online, and getting it dirt cheap when there was no interest in it at auction, probably due to the lack of water rights. The stories of his meanness and tough-guy image were legion.

Consequently, I had pocketed my handgun which I usually carry with me anyway. Most of my firepower is kept under lock and key at my bungalow, unless I need a specific weapon for a specific job.

He stood on his porch, shotgun in hand as I got out of my truck. "Guess you can't read too good, can you?"

I assumed he referred to the trespassing signs. "I don't consider myself a trespasser," I said, but I didn't move in any closer.

Buford Thomas is a short man, five-seven or eight, maybe, but you don't think of him as short, because every muscle in his body is sinewy and he's built for strength. Everything about him is angular and hard, and he looked at me with his eyes tilted, and a square jaw and head at an angle, too.

"You're on my land, you're trespassing." It was a simple conclusion for him.

"My name is Jimmy O'Reilly," I said.

"I know who you are."

" I'm licensed by the State of Kansas to investigate crimes, and I have a few questions I'd like to ask you in regards to Vernon Johnson's death." There had been a constant snarling since I arrived, and when I looked off to the side of the house, four Rottweilers stood chained to metal stakes at twenty foot intervals. They all drooled, with their legs spread wide and heads lowered as they snarled away at me.

"I didn't like the man. I'm not sorry to hear he's dead. And I don't care what kind of license you got, get out of here before I commence to firing." He raised the barrel of the shotgun slightly, still pointed off to the side, but he made his statement with the motion.

"Do you keep pigs on your place, Mr. Thomas?" He didn't bother to respond. "What I heard is, you and Vernon Johnson had words about your illegal activity of siphoning water off the river." I nodded toward the stack of pipes and couplings.

"Johnson and me had more than words. He was an old fool and he deserves to rot in that north field of his until buzzards strip him of his innards. He was a creature of routine, and all creatures of routine are fools. And what my activities are is none of your business."

Out past the dogs I saw a pile of bones. I couldn't tell from where I stood if they were human or not, but I could make out a rib cage and skull among them.

"Mr. Thomas, I see the shotgun in your hand, but I should tell you, my license permits me to carry a firearm, which I do, and it allows me to defend myself with deadly force." My Ruger SP101 sat snug in its pocket holster and I slid my hand into my jean's pocket. I'd had a lot of practice at the firing range shooting through a pocket. "Now, would you care to tell me what that pile of bones is out there beyond your dogs?"

"I don't care to tell you shit." He leveled the shotgun at me.

Well, that shows you what counterforce and bluffing will buy you. Squat. I felt my neck muscles tightening. I thought better of doing anything with my Ruger, so I walked around to the driver's side of my truck, putting it between me and Buford Thomas, and addressed him over the top of the cab. "Those bones may make you a person of interest in a possible homicide. You sure you don't want to discuss them with me before the police arrive?"

He pumped the fore-end of his twelve-gauge and chambered a shell.

"No, I guess you don't." I climbed in my truck and slowly backed out the drive, his shotgun following me as I went.

Phil poured himself a cup of coffee out of a Silex as I burst through the door of the station.
"You know those bones you denied knowing anything about?" I said.
He set the Silex down and turned to me, cup in hand.
"Well, you need to get out to Buford Thomas' place, because he's got a heap of them in his side yard. Skull, rib cage, and whole lot more."
Phil's eyes got wide and he set his cup down, but didn't say anything.
"Start earning your keep. I'll check back later on what you found." Then I stormed out.

I drove back to Vernon Johnson's farm and walked out to the north field again. The edge of the field touched the south side of Buford Thomas' farm. Buford had clear access to the Johnson's acreage without going around and through town on the roads, as I had. He could have come and gone at will with nobody knowing.
I looked around and suddenly realized that the tractor was now upright. I had no idea how Phil, or somebody else for that matter, accomplished this feat, but the tractor had been righted and sat in the sun, its faded red nose pointing back away from the river now. The muddy area had dried, but curiously, the footprints were no longer there. The area was all smoothed over.
I'd searched every place I could think of in the immediate area, not really knowing what I was looking for, and was about to give up when I looked off in the distance toward where the tractor pointed. The lapis turtle was a knot against my thigh, as if prodding me to remember, and I thought of something Bob had shown me once when we

were kids. He wasn't supposed to, because it was a family secret of sorts, but when we were playing and roaming the fields one day, he took me to a small opening in a hill far back behind the farmhouse. The opening was hidden, partially because of size and position, but also because of a large stone that stood a few feet in front of it. It was an optical illusion, so that unless you were behind the stone, it looked like part of the hill and it camouflaged the entrance.

It took me awhile to find it, and there was a fair amount of brush grown up around it now so I had to pull some of it back and away. But there was evidence of recent activity, because a narrow passage had been cut through a portion of the vegetation. Then I walked back to my truck to get a flashlight and my camera and flash attachment.

When I finally ducked my head and entered, it was just as I remembered, a small stone enclosure within the side of the hill. It was dark and cool inside, and a damp, sweet smell of moisture clinging to limestone walls soothed me. Bob's grandparents had used it as a spring house and for cold storage before rural electricity was brought to the area.

I switched on my flashlight, and there they were on the stone floor off to one side. The bones. I walked over and shined my light on them. They did exist and they were human, there was no doubt about that. Some parts of the skeleton were still connected, while other individual bones lay singly. I took a few pictures as an evidentiary precaution, and driving back into town, I pondered the significance of the possibility of two sets of bones, each located on adjoining parcels of land. As hidden as these bones were, there was no telling who might know about them or what might happen to them.

I knew who I had to call and I knew it needed to be done right away.

8

"O'Reilly, you son-of-a-bitch, where have you been?"
"Laura. How'd you know it was me?"
"Caller ID, you idiot. Don't you have caller ID?"
"You know me better than that, Laura."
I hadn't talked to Laura Bascome in two, maybe three years. As usual, with Laura, I was at a loss for words. I decided to cut straight to the chase.
"I have a favor to ask, Laura."
"You don't call for three years and then, out of the blue, you have a favor to ask. I don't think so. Alright, ask. But first, recite some poetry."
"What?"
"You heard me. No favors requested unless you give up some great verse."
"Okay, here goes," I said. I was thinking back to the Yeats poem Janie talked about earlier, and I recited.
"Come, let me sing into your ear; those dancing days are

gone, and all that silk and satin gear; Crouch upon a stone…"

"Oh, Yeats, Jimmy. You're quoting Yeats. You are a wonder. I wish you would sing into my ear, or at least take me dancing."

"No you don't, and quit saying that. Here's my favor. I need you to come up to Chisholm and look at some bones."

Laura was a bone expert. We had run together, part of what we all called the gang-of-five, back in our college days at Wichita State University. Then, she went off to Chicago, did police beat work like me, graduated to homicide, and earned a PhD in anthropology. She returned to the Midwest several years ago when her mother took ill, and now she teaches courses in criminal justice at WSU. She also happens to be big into Aikido as well as hold a Distinguished Expert rating for marksmanship. A real Renaissance gal.

"Look at some bones, huh? I could do that, O'Reilly, but it'll cost you."

"Cost me what? You want dinner? I'll cook for you, you know I'm good."

"I come at a higher price. I want you to take me dancing. Oh Jimmy, those dancing days are gone. Ha. Got you on that one."

Back in college, the five of us who ran around together would go to every kind of dance we could find. Rock and roll, C and W, early heavy metal or acid rock, you name it. But Laura loved country and western. "You still like line dancing?" I asked.

"You know it."

"I don't know how a bone doctor could be into country and western, but there's a dance out at the Knights of Columbus Hall Thursday. You come up, read these bones for me and the treat's on me."

"I have a mid-morning class tomorrow. Shall we say, one o'clock? And I'm holding you to your promise on dancing."

At precisely one in the afternoon, Laura Bascome pulled into my drive in her 1957 vintage Venetian Red Corvette with hard top removed. The long auburn hair she usually had pulled back in a bun when in front of her classes was down and tangled from the wind. She was wearing a tailored, camel color knee-length skirt and matching suit jacket and pumps. She was slim and fine-looking for a woman in her mid-forties, in shape from her martial arts regimen, and the fact that she herself knew it showed in her walk. I went out on the front porch to greet her and she gave me big hug.

"I hate to tell you this, Laura, but the bones aren't just sitting around in my living room on display. You're going to have to cross some farmland."

"I brought a change. You know me, I have to travel in style."

"Still keeping up with the Aikido training?" She is a sixth Dan in Aikido.

She just looked at me with her patented deadpan stare. Laura has a slight build, but I've seen her use an Aikido throw to toss a man three times her size across a room and into a wall with bone-crushing results.

"Well, run in and change and then we'll hop in my truck. We need to be a little less conspicuous than your screaming red machine you're driving."

She got a duffle bag out of her car, went in to change and emerged a few minutes later ready for field work. Well, sort of: Polo denims and Vasque hiking boots.

"You sure keep a lot of fire power under lock and key for someone who just does skip trace work."

She had seen my gun cabinet. "Remnants of the old days," I said. "Before I took down my P.I. shingle."

"An array of handguns, a Remington M24, assault rifles and both 12 and 20 gauge shotguns? You expecting to quash a rebellion or start one?"

I didn't tell her anything about the case as we drove out. We just talked about old college days and the other three members of the gang-of-five, all of us CJ majors. Except they called it AJ back in those days. Administration of Justice. Ed is a police chief in a small Oklahoma town now, Jack always was and still is a beat cop in Oklahoma City, and Bonnie, the other female, now did administrative work for the Kansas City, Missouri Department of Corrections. We were all still in the business, one way or the other. Back then, in the seventies, we all just ran together. The dances. Afternoon beers at Kirby's on Seventeenth Street across from the U. No romantic involvement. Just good friends having good times together.

When we got to Johnson's farm, Laura didn't ask about the crime tape still strung across the drive and around the yard. She moved with the grace of an Aikido master as we crossed the field. We entered the spring house opening and I shined my flashlight on the bones. She didn't say anything. She circled them, then squatted from several different perspectives looking more closely, but she didn't touch or move them. Then she finally spoke.

"Here's what I can tell you from a first observation, that's with no lab work, of course. This is a female. White. From the development, growth stage and joint fusion, I would say she was perhaps late teens at the time of death. There is no immediate indication of blunt force trauma."

She took out a measuring device and laid it next to what looked like a leg bone. She referred to it as a humerus, then said, "She was between five-four and five-seven. As you can see, much of the skeleton is intact, but there is some, although minimal, disarticulation. This is somewhat surprising, though not necessarily an anomaly, because the bleaching of the bones indicates considerable exposure to the elements."

"You mean," I asked, "with that kind of exposure, animals would normally scatter and, as you put it, disarticulate the bones?"

"Exactly. In addition, all major bones seem to be present, but with two hundred and six bones in the human body it is difficult, without lab reconstruction, to account for what might be missing. There is one curious aspect though."

She stood up, stepped back and paused for a moment.

"Both the left and right hands are present and articulated with each radius, but the index finger of the left hand is missing."

"What's the significance of that?" I asked.

"Maybe nothing. Maybe this person lost it in an accident previous to death. Then again, who knows?"

"How long has she been dead?"

"I don't know. Do you know how long the remains have been here?"

"Not long. They were found on the bank of the Little Arkansas, maybe a week or so ago, and then, I presume, brought here."

"Any idea who she might be?"

"None."

"One reasonable conjecture," she explained, "is, that if they were indeed found on the river, they may have originated upstream at some point and for whatever reason, and then over the years were brought farther and farther downstream with rains and flooding, perhaps protected beneath water surface at times, perhaps exposed at others. With the amount of bleaching from exposure, there could be anywhere from five years to twenty or thirty years interval from the time of death."

"There is another complication for your consideration," I said. "There may be a second set of bones." I explained the pile I'd seen at Buford's.

"We have access to those?"

"Not at the present, but I let a local deputy know about them, for all the good that will do."

As we drove back into town, she asked me the question I'm sure had been on her mind for some time since she'd initially crossed the crime scene tape. "You have authorization for us to be out there?"

"Nope."

Then she followed with, "Who knows the bones are there?"

"As far I know, just you and me."

"O'Reilly, you big Irish thug, you."

"Irish-American," I corrected her. "Fifth generation."

Back at the house sitting in her red Corvette, she put on her RayBan shades, tossed her hair with a flick of the head and reminded me with some degree of verbal force, "Thursday. I'm holding you to your end of the deal. Don't try to bail on me. I know a good skip tracer that'll hunt you down."

9

Face-time with Phil again. The only question was whether to seek him out personally or to start with his boss, Sheriff Alexander. That question was settled for me on Tuesday when I walked through the door of the low, blond brick offices and local jail on Commercial, just north of the town square.

"Phil."

"Jimmy."

Our greetings were often as short as our names around here.

"Is Alex around?"

"No, he and Mavis took off for Florida. Two weeks vacation. Gone deep sea fishing in Fort Myers on the Gulf Coast." His squat body sat behind the desk, a heavy stomach bulging into the front edge of it. He made no move to rise.

I took a chair from the waiting area, scraped it across the faded squares of linoleum floor and sat down next to his desk.

"I'm having some problems with certain aspects of Vernon Johnson's death," I began."

"How so?" He studied me with a steady and practiced eye.

"Well, some things just don't square with the facts. For example, there is just no good reason that he was out in the fields on his tractor at that particular time on a Sunday morning."

"I told you to ask Bob about that."

"And I told you, you're doing a piss-poor job by not asking him yourself." I felt my neck muscles starting to tighten.

"No need to raise these kind of questions on an accidental death. It only bothers the family."

"Your concern is touching, Phil." I let the "accidental death" part slide for the moment. "Then there's the issue of what he was wearing. If he was out doing field work, he would not have been wearing his leisure suit. In addition, he was wearing it early the day before his death, and that was the last time Bob, or anyone we know of, saw him."

"You know Jimmy, Vernon was old and old people's minds can't be accounted for sometimes. I don't see that what he was wearing has any bearing on this."

"What happened to those footprints that were in Johnson's north field by the tractor?" I decided to see how he'd react to this one.

"Footprints? What footprints you talking about?"

"The ones that disappeared mysteriously."

He stood up and waddled around the desk, looking down at me with his hands on his hips. "I don't know what you're talking about."

I stood and fulfilled my prophecy of face-time. "How'd that Massey Ferguson get upright? And while we are on the subject of strange occurrences, you still haven't said word-one about the bones Bob told you about." I didn't mention what I'd discovered in the spring house.

His eyes flicked off to the side for just an instant, and then he was back in my face. "I'm telling you Jimmy, you've gone loco."

"You checked out Buford's place yet for those bones I told you about?" I felt the mastoid and capitis muscles knotting in my neck and I started flexing my jaw.

"No, but I intend to get out there soon."

"Phil?" I asked, my nose almost touching his, "Are you stonewalling me?"

"Stonewalling?" His puffy face got red and he pointed a fat finger into my washboard stomach. "You listen here, Jimmy…"

"No, you listen," I said. He held his finger with his other hand now. I think he hurt it on my stomach. "Why did you have Doc Smally sign the death certificate as natural causes if you think it was an accident?"

"How do you know–" He caught himself mid-question. "It's a question of the chicken or the egg. Which came first? Did the heart attack kill him and cause the tractor to turn over on him, or vice-a-versy? There's no way to tell and one theory's just as valid as the other."

"As long as you're coming up with theories, you got one on where Doc Smally might be?"

Phil's eyes flicked again. "I imagine he's at his office."

"His office is locked, he's left town and stood his patients up, but you managed to find him on Sunday morning. What do you know about that?" The mastoids and capitis were starting to form a cord and I knew a full blown headache was near, if not a total immobilization of the neck.

"I don't know nothin'."

"You're just like the old song, aren't you? 'Don't know nothin' 'bout nothin' at all.' Well, I'll tell you one thing. I know 'one and one makes two,' but nothing's adding up here."

I got out of his face and started to leave, and then turned back to him. "You know, you remind me of a turtle, Phil."

"How so?" He looked indignant.

"You're always blowing it out your ass."

"What the hell?" He blustered and got red in the face again.

"That's how sea turtles breathe, through their butt. A little known curiosity of the species." I smiled. "Well, we'll know a little more after the autopsy, won't we?" I slipped that in at the end and kept grinning.

"Ain't gonna be one, not with a natural death…"

But I had already turned and was out the door, leaving him to figure it out and not bothering to raise the aspect of the bones again.

I drove north out of town trying to cool down and flexing my neck and jaw. I always tend to lose it when I go face to face with people like Phil, and I needed to come back down from it.

But I had something else in mind, too. If Vernon left Chisholm this same way on Saturday, it must have been for a reason. Maybe it was to go to Buford's. But with a second set of bones now discovered, I wasn't so sure. What was out here other than the wheat? Did anyone see him after Ter Junior?

I drove several miles and pulled off on the shoulder at a crossroad. Nothing around but wheat, ripening in the June sun. Not even any activity in the fields as it would still be a few days before the custom cutters arrived. A maintainer was running his Cat down the county road, scraping the hard-packed surface level, but he wouldn't have been out here on a Saturday to observe anything. I flagged him down anyway and shouted over his idling engine.

"You seen anything out here in the last week or so? Any unusual activity? Anyone around who normally isn't?"

"No. Same ole, same ole." His diesel sputtered some black smoke and he scraped his way on down the road.

I pulled the blue lapis out of my pocket and it sat warm in my palm. Suddenly, the image of Phil's eyes flicking came to me and I had a strange feeling about the spring house set of bones. I drove back through town, then east out to the Johnson place, parked at the gravel drive and walked out to the spring house cave. The bones were gone.

As I emerged through the opening into daylight and started to round the stone that hid the entrance, a shot rang out and a round chipped the side of the stone. White powder rose off of it as I ducked back behind, crouched and reached for my Ruger. I waited, Ruger in hand. A minute later I could hear an engine start and a vehicle take off down the county road.

10

In light of my recent conversation with Phil, I figured reporting the shooting incident might be counterproductive, so I drove back to my house instead.

My house, that wood frame bungalow that sits on the west end of Chisholm at the edge of the wheat field, was a Sears and Roebuck catalogue kit. In the 1920s my grandparents ordered it, had the kit delivered by rail and then built it themselves. My parents lived in it for a number of years, then it sat empty after they both passed, so when my wife died and I decided to quit the force, it seemed natural to come back here. I'd had a little brother, younger than me by two years, who died of a childhood illness when he was eight. So there was just me left, and it seemed the right thing to do to restore the old family home. The sweat and hard grunt work it took to reclaim it from a toll exacted by neglect and abandonment helped me forget the pain of my wife's death that I was going through at the time.

In the morning I would have to drive into Wichita on a skip trace job, so I poured myself a glass of red and kicked back on the terrace to look out over the field. The wheat was ready, but cutters hadn't gotten this far north yet, so the dull gold shafts stood heavy in the humid air.

"Ty." I called out into the fading evening light.

I hadn't seen Tiresias anywhere, but then, he couldn't see me either. Still, we both knew each other was there, and I think he saw more in his sightless world than I saw in my sighted one. I felt the blue lapis in my pocket and wondered if Ty had buried himself in the sand pit I made for him or crawled under the hollow log I'd set out for protection or hid somewhere in the herbs.

The air itself was heavy. Heat and humidity combined to weigh down and suppress lung capacity, so breathing was shallow and my temples ached from a change in barometric pressure. My neck muscles were still corded from my encounter with Phil. The wine helped a little, but talcum powder I applied that morning had a dank smell to it, and sweat trickled down my armpits. The air was still, like being in a vacuum with all life sucked out of it. Out to the west big cumulus clouds puffed up, and I knew we might get hit full force tonight with winds and pelting rain, or it might go around us with nothing but the heat and sweat and dead-still, breathlessness of the vacuum remaining. Such were the vagaries of Kansas weather.

The wheat waited, but so did the farmers, both in anticipation. But then again, so did I. In the end, it all dissipated, falling apart in a lifeless, formless pastiche of clouds before it got to us.

Wednesday morning I left on a skip trace job for Bomber Jackson. This was, after all, how I currently earned my living. Bomber runs Air Capitol Bail Bonds down on South Seneca in Wichita, and takes his nickname from a previous incarnation as a line-worker in the military division of Wichita's aircraft industry. I take assignments from a number of bondsman, but Bomber gives me steady jobs, and this one, like many of his, should have been easy. Should have.

As I headed down I-35 toward Wichita I passed a couple of cutters who had worked their way up from Oklahoma and were starting on fields that had ripened. I thought about what an asshole Phil was and if he was dirty or not. All the possibilities played themselves out in my mind. As it turned out, I would have been better off to concentrate on my task at hand.

Unlike many of my jobs, I had to actually bring this guy in. It still should have been easy. Fortunately, he was well-known in the world I trafficked in and easily available. Known on the street as Slapstick, he was a habitual wife-slash-girlfriend beater, I emphasize the slash part, and I only had to go to his usual address on West Pawnee to find him. Bringing him in turned out to be another matter.

I usually have my Ruger in a shoulder holster on these kinds of jobs, mainly for show. I hardly ever use it. But it was parked inside my push-button cutaway, under the dashboard, because my mind had been wandering and I hadn't given any thought to the job at hand. So I parked outside Slapstick's apartment sans gun, sans bravado, sans a whole lot of thought, really, since I had been doting mainly on Phil, and that proved to be a mistake.

Slapstick came out of a ground-floor apartment heading toward his rusted-out blue Chevelle.

"John," I called out. I couldn't bring myself to call him Slapstick to his face. "John, Bomber needs to talk to you."

At that precise moment his live-in walked out and headed toward the Chevelle. She was short and chubby and pale-skinned, and she walked up and rested next to his skinny, tattooed-lined body like a spider's egg in its half-hung web.

He rung his spidery arm around her pudgy neck and her tongue flapped out. "Get the fuck outta here or she goes down," he said. He pulled what looked like a hunter's knife out from inside his boot.

My heart sank. It's always the innocent and unknowing that get caught in the cross-fire. Then again, maybe she wasn't innocent and maybe she wasn't unknowing. "John, you only have to appear on a misdemeanor possession." I didn't mention this was a third time on two previous failures to appear. I figured as fried as his brain was, he probably wouldn't remember.

That's when she craned her neck and bit his thumb, hard. He howled and dropped his little egg. She took off running toward me with him following, knife in hand. I opened my truck door and grabbed a baseball bat I keep there, just in time to use it to deflect his knife arm. Then I kneed him to the stomach and he crumpled like cellophane off a corsage. I clapped the cuffs on him and hauled him down to Bomber's on South Seneca. End of skip trace job.

I'd disposed of Slapstick, but Phil wouldn't leave my mind so easily. When I got back to Chisholm, I stopped to see Bob and LaVonda with more questions. Tick greeted me on the front porch by not moving, but just lifting his eyes mournfully. He missed Vernon as much as all of us did.

Their shades were pulled and it was dark in the unlit living room. They sat on their couch, each on the edge of it, with me opposite in a wingback chair.

"Have the two of you given any thought to the arrangements?"

Bob looked over at LaVonda, who sat quietly shaking her head. "We... I mean me and LaVonda... we been thinking Saturday morning, or maybe Sunday afternoon, if we get permission after the autopsy."

I could see they were still struggling with the initial grief and it was difficult for me to prod like I had to. "I do have to ask more questions. I hope you don't mind."

"You go right on ahead," said LaVonda. "You do what you have to do."

"Can you think of anything else Vernon might have said that could relate to any of what has happened? Especially about those bones?"

Bob thought for a moment. "No, I can't."

"Bob." LaVonda spoke tentatively. "Remember what you said about ... you know."

"It's just that he was so obsessed about them and he went on and on, and I believed him, but I sort of tuned a lot of it out after awhile."

"Bob." LaVonda prodded him some more.

"Well, he told me he had some good news, at least he thought it would be good, to deliver to someone, but he wouldn't say who and he let on like he knew whose bones they were, but by then I just wasn't listening anymore."

"And that other thing, too," said LaVonda.

"I don't see where's that'd make any difference at all, LaVonda."

She just stared at him until he said, "Oh, alright." He walked into the dining room. I heard a door open and close and he returned with a large box.

"He give me these, Dad did, he said for safekeeping. But I don't know who'd even want them."

I opened the box and it was filled with flyers and programs from dances and song nights from the old Grange Hall and the Knights of Columbus Hall and other local places. They went back, maybe twenty-five or thirty years.

"If it's okay with you, I'm going to take these with me, Bob. I promise I'll take good care of them. And I want you to know one other thing, some good news. I found the bones. Vernon was right about them."

Bob suddenly got animated and wanted to see them right away, so I tried to calm him down by telling him that the bad news was they had disappeared, but that only got him more excited.

"Bob, you need to calm down and let me see if I can tie any of this together. And remember. Don't let Phil know about any of this and tell me if he comes asking more questions."

Back on my terrace that night, with the Catholics and the Methodists ensconced in their respective Wednesday night services, I silently sipped my red, and thought how all cowards like Slapstick and Phil hide behind their veneer of stupidity or lack of knowledge, and pretend they know nothing of what is going on. Lack of knowledge seemed to validate their reality and relieve them of responsibility. I was ashamed of my own inability to deal with such individuals.

It was late and it was dark, and the June bugs crawling on my terrace flagstones and swirling in the light that spilled from the house seemed inured to the heaviness of the humid air my lungs labored with. I breathed heavily, and the fact that these June bugs were once slimy grub worms, but now were still just as annoying in their new life and form, was lost on me. Either way, worm or bug, at least they provided Ty something to eat.

11

Thursday morning I drove my pickup down to Commercial, rumbling over the old uneven red bricks. I passed a tractor coming up the middle of the street, and parked outside the dry goods store. I couldn't bring myself to call it a department store. Dry goods was what I'd always known it as. Alice, the clerk who has worked there as long as I can remember, wrapped my purchase in brown paper and was in the process of tying it neatly with butcher's string.

"Do you know when Vernon's services will be?" she asked in a voice quavering with age, not uncertainty.

"No, Alice, I don't," I said. "We'll all just have to wait until Bob and LaVonda let us know."

"Well, I hope those protestors don't show up. That would be a disgrace."

"Protestors? What are you talking about?"

"You know, those crazies from Topeka who go around protesting at soldiers' funerals."

"I haven't heard anything about that, Alice. But I don't think anyone would want to dishonor a World War II hero."

"I hope not. You let me know when you hear about the funeral arrangements," she said. And then she added, "Do you suppose Betty Chalmers will have the mettle to show up at it?"

I stared at her, again having no idea what she was talking about.

"Oops." She slid the package across to me and started away.

"What do you mean, oops?"

"Nothing."

"Alice, you don't say something like that and then dismiss it with 'nothing.'"

"I just thought, with you investigating and all, you would know about it." I stared at her some more. "Well, you know, they were sweet on each other. Been seeing each other in the evenings now and then."

"Alice, Vernon was seventy-nine and Betty's close to that herself."

"So. I'm close to that myself, too, and it doesn't keep me from having a little fun."

"Shame on you, Alice." I smiled when I said it, and she blushed.

"Well, it's not like they were trying to hide it. They just didn't tell anybody but me. Where you wearing that fancy shirt you bought to, anyways?"

"I got a hot date myself, Alice." I winked at her and then walked out with my package of a red plaid western shirt for tonight's dance under my arm. It had fake, or is that faux, pearl buttons and black trim around the pockets. I still had a bolo somewhere, if I could find it, and my boots and straw hat were in my closet, unused for many years. I intended to keep my verbal contractual deal with Laura, and I meant to do it in some degree of style.

I tossed the parcel in the pickup and started back to see Alice again. I had one more question for her. But when I turned around, Buford Thomas stood face to chest with me. His face, my chest. He pushed me back against the side panel of my truck and pinned me with one of his muscle-knotted arms. I probably could have freed myself, but I didn't resist.

"What the hell you think you're doing calling the police out to my place?"

"I told you, Buford, you are now a person of interest in a possible murder investigation. What did you expect when you refused to talk with me?"

He stepped back and squared off, like he was getting ready to throw a punch at me, so I stood up straight and glared down at him, ready to counter his punch.

"You so much as set foot on my place again, I'll come after you, and it won't be with that scattergun of mine. It'll be with one of my hunting knives." He turned and strode off across Commercial.

Buford didn't know it, but he just issued an invitation to me for a return visit. It's hard to refuse such congeniality.

I saw Phil rounding the corner toward the alley entrance to the station. He eyed me and quickened his step, but I cut him off before he made it.

"I understand you paid a call to Buford Thomas," I said. "What'd you find out?"

"Deer bones."

"Deer bones? You saying that skull and ribcage were part of a deer skeleton?"

"That's what Buford said."

"You mean you didn't look at them?"

"I took the man at his word," said Phil, and walked away, leaving me itching all the more for that invitation to a revisit.

First things first, though. I thought about what Alice told me. Betty Chalmers lived north of town. Suddenly, Buford's place wasn't the only one that had significance, and north of town took on a whole new meaning.

"Land sakes, Mr. O'Reilly. We weren't keeping it a secret or anything. We just didn't advertise it. It cost money to take out an ad." She laughed at her own joke.

"Something like that is pretty difficult to keep secret in a town like Chisholm."

"Well, Vernon just came out here of an evening and we sat and talked and listened to music, and I would play some on the guitar and he would too. Nothing fancy, mind you, just simple pleasures. His wife, Addy, passed some eight years ago, and my Henry passed near twenty years back. Vernon and me were both pretty lonely, and we were good company for each other. Talking, singing and playing. That's all."

We sat in the living room of her farm house north of Chisholm, one very similar to Vernon's nineteenth century home. The rooms were small, and even sparsely furnished, they seemed crowded. She sat straight-backed and prim, with her hands folded in her lap.

"I'm sorry he's no longer with us. He was a good friend to me. I'm sorry he's not here for you anymore, too."

"I will miss him something fierce, Mr. O'Reilly. Is it true you think he was murdered?"

"I'm just asking some questions right now, Betty, and I'd like to ask you a few, too, if that's okay." She nodded a silent approval. "Was Vernon coming to see you Saturday morning?"

"No, not that I know of. We really only got together in the evenings, like I say, to chat and listen to old records, sing and play. I still have a 45 player and it can change speeds and even play old 33s."

"Why else might he have wanted to come out north of town on Saturday?"

"No reason I could think of. Unless he was going to one of those dance halls, like the Grange. We talked about the old acts that use to play the dance halls. I used to go to them all. We even went to a dance together a few months ago just to listen. He especially liked guitar and fiddle music. A couple of weeks ago he asked me if I remembered some young musician a few years back, which I didn't, but I got out my old programs. I saved every one and kept them in a box. I gave them all to Vernon. Maybe he just wanted to go out and reminisce."

"Well, I'll take my leave of you now, Betty, if you don't mind."

"Wait," she said. "I want to do something for you, so maybe you will understand." She brought out an old, plain guitar. "This here's an old pawn shop guitar. No acoustics to speak of, but it's what we played, Vernon and me, of an evening. I'd play a song and then he would. We took turns."

She strummed a few chords and she had me hooked, and then she picked a lead-line melody from some old standard I couldn't name. "I won't sing for you, 'cause I'm not too good. Vernon, he liked a real pure voice."

"Thank you, Betty," I said. "That was beautiful."

"Vernon would have liked it, too," she said. "Mr. O'Reilly, am I a suspect?"

"I'm not the police, Betty. I'm just asking a few questions is all."

"But do you think the police might suspect me?"

"The police always suspect everybody. That's part of their job. But I don't think you have anything to worry about."

"I did have a motive, you know."

I looked at her incredulously. "Motive? You?"

"Yes." She looked down, shame-faced. "Vernon changed his will recently, and well, he is leaving me his Gibson." Then she whispered confidentially, "I don't think any of the family know about it."

"Gibson? You mean, as in guitar?"

"That's right. He had an old Gibson guitar he'd bring over sometimes when we sang and played in the evenings. I don't have a pure voice, but I sure could make that thing sing. You see, that Gibson is probably worth several thousand dollars. I once told Alice, she knew about Vernon and me, I told her I would kill to own an instrument like that. I didn't mean it literally, though."

I assured Betty again she needn't worry, but back at my truck I shook my head in disbelief at all I was finding out. I looked down at the box of programs I put in the cab behind the passenger seat. It was time to keep my promise to Bob and LaVonda and put them someplace safe.

Late that afternoon, after spending a couple of hours doing computer searches for upcoming skip trace jobs, I decided to forgo my usual kitchen efforts, walk into town, and have me a greasy burrito at Dottie's, a sort of pre fixe culinary delight before my commitment to Laura for the evening. It was one of my few guilty pleasures I allowed myself, occasionally.

I was on my way back, hoofing it down Fourth Street, when the front blew through and the barometric pressure plummeted. I knew it, even before the winds got to me, because I heard the intermittent clang of the metal monkey ring against its pole on the grade school playground three blocks away. That sound was always my barometer.

The air still hung heavy with humidity where I was, and then the front arrived. Winds picked up suddenly. Elm branches whirled overhead. I found myself leaning into the west wind as I walked up my drive and saw the front door open. Inside, I looked out on the terrace and there was

Janie, arms outstretched, hair blowing in the wind and twirling around and around in circles.

"Janie," I said, "What are you doing?" The wind was picking up strength and getting even louder.

"I'm dancing in the wind," she yelled.

"What?"

"Dancing in the wind." She screamed over the roar, then came inside closing my French doors. "You know, like the Yeats' poem. I read the one called 'To a Child Dancing in the Wind." I like it better than the one about dancing days being gone. It's happier, like what dancing should really be about. So I was tumbling out my hair and ignoring the wind's roar, just like it says in the poem. Cool, huh?"

I was about to comment on how dangerous it was, considering that lighting flickered in the distance, when Laura's 'Vette pulled in the drive. She walked through the front door dressed to the hilt, full cowgirl regalia, tight black pants, bright red western shirt with snap buttons, real pearl, wide black sleeves at the wrist and black stitching on the collar and pockets. She wore a red felt hat, and red and black leather-tooled cowgirl boots.

Janie's jaw dropped and her eyes got big. "Wow," she said, and then stood mute.

I introduced them and told Janie where we were going.

"Way to go, Mr. 'O.'" She winked at me.

"Janie, Laura and I are just good friends."

"Yeah, sure."

"Look," I said, "I'm going to change. You two get to know each other, and I'll be back in a minute."

"Mr. 'O.' I kind of like that. Do you mind if I call you that?"

"Not at all, Janie."

"Well, Mr. 'O,' I was looking through your CDs trying to find some good music to play. Do you have any Eminem?"

"I eat M&Ms, Janie, I don't listen to them."

She got a puzzled look on her face and I realized I was being my usual obtuse self, so I just said, "No I don't, I'm sorry. But help yourself to anything that's there."

"Don't you have anything besides that Indian music?" she asked.

"Indian music?" Now I was puzzled.

"Yeah. All those CDs by some group called The Chieftains."

I left to change, not wanting to comment on her remark, and when I returned in my red plaid shirt, she and Laura were deep in conversation, oblivious to my new shirt or my old bolo, worn boots and crumpled hat.

"Mr. 'O,' I finished my chores earlier, but would you mind if I stayed a while longer while you two are out dancing?"

Laura shot me a glance.

"Not at all. Make yourself at home, Janie."

After a pause, Laura said, "Janie's mother is entertaining a… a gentleman caller this evening."

Then Janie said, "He's weird. I don't feel too comfortable being around him."

"Stay as long as you like, Janie. We'll be back late, but make yourself at home. You might try some of that, ah… Indian music. See what you think of it."

"Would it be okay if I brought Ty in to keep him company. He stared through the French doors earlier, like maybe he could sense what was going on in here, like he was lonely or something."

"That's probably not a good idea. Turtles need to stay acclimated to their environment, and Tiresias is pretty much a loner anyway."

"Okay. It just seems sort of sad, him being blind and all. It's like he doesn't have any friends."

"I think there's some creatures that just prefer it that way, Janie."

With that, Laura and I headed out the door, got in my gun-rack-empty pickup, and drove to the Knights of Columbus Hall north of town.

12

The crushed gravel parking lot was filled with pickups, except each one had at least one firearm in its rear window, a stark contrast to my empty rack. Couples sidled up to each other, leaning next to their vehicles, both males and females with long neck bottles of Bud in their hands. Twangie fiddle music, strains of "Your Faded Love," drifted out the open door into the air, now calm and cooler since the front blew through, but with lightning still flickering far off in the distance.

The hall was a low, square cinderblock building, painted a dingy gray on the exterior. Inside, the décor was retro-minimalist. A plain cement floor stretched almost uninterrupted from wall to wall. The walls themselves had coarsely painted vegetation on them, some sort of a flowering vine that twisted its way upward. Interspersed here and there, randomly, were white plastic trellises with plastic pastel colored flowers and vines wired to them. Off to one side was a thick and heavy bar, its front covered in black vinyl, and its top, laminated Formica with a fake wood grain. In the center of the floor a keg sat iced down in a giant plastic trash barrel, and a line of would-be drinkers waited to suck their drafts into sixteen ounce plastic cups. All told, plastic seemed to rule the design concept and I doubted anyone involved watched HGTV.

After grabbing a couple of drafts, Laura and I found a small table close to the bandstand with, of course, a plastic tablecloth. A term which I believe to be an oxymoron. It had water rings from the previous tenants' drinks. The bandstand itself consisted of unpainted plywood nailed on top of some two-by-sixes. But the band rocked. If a country and western band can rock, that is. I stood and offered my hand.

"Lady, will you walk about with your friend?"

"Quit quoting Shakespeare, O'Reilly. Talk plain. Come on, let's cut a rug."

We danced all the line dances and country swing they played, which was considerable, sat out the new dances neither of us knew, watched while young ones did some sort of pushy-tush thing, and quietly sipped our suds on the weepy ballads.

Laura wiped a tear away at the end of a faithful rendition of Hank Williams' "I'm So Lonesome I Could Cry," and said, "Sorry. It gets to me every time I hear it."

"No apology needed, 'Mam," I said in my mock accent. I grabbed her arm and pulled her back out to the dance floor as the band jumped into a rendition of "Great Balls in Cowtown." While we boogied, we politely argued over the precise meaning of the word "balls" in the title, until I noticed her attention shift to the band. In particular, the fiddle player, the one member who did not fit the traditionalist makeup of the group. In his early twenties, and of course I know for a fact that Laura has an affinity for younger men, he was junior by twenty to forty years more than any of the other members. His hair was long and stringy, although neatly pulled back, and he sported a scraggly Fu-Manchu beard and mustache. He wore black baggy cargo pants and a black tee-shirt that said "Spear Britney," and had an unbuttoned long-sleeved flannel shirt over it. His feet were ensconced in giant clod-hopper Doc Martens boots. But he played a mean fiddle.

"'Mam," I mocked again. "I'm considerin' requesting 'Your Cheating Heart,' if'n you all keep this up." I nodded toward the fiddle player.

She suddenly stopped dancing and said, "Go get me another beer, then I've got something to tell you."

"Oh, great. Left on the dance floor and jilted again." I smiled and walked over to the keg. When I returned to the table with her beer, she sat there, still staring at the kid on stage. "What's the attraction? The Fu-Manchu?"

"Look at his fiddle," she said, not taking her eyes off of him. "What do you notice?"

"I don't know. I wouldn't know a fiddle from a violin," I said, deadpan serious.

She rolled her eyes at me. "Funny. I'm talking about its construction. The four tuning pegs which are always made of wood, almost always ebony."

"Well, one of his isn't, but what's the big deal?"

"It's a phalanx."

I looked at her with a dumb expression, I'm sure, as my mind conjured up a military image of hundreds of these little white things on a hillside getting ready to attack an opposing army's phalanx of other little white things.

"A bone, you bonehead. It's a finger-bone, a phalanx."

"Oh, that kind of phalanx. Only you would notice that."

"That was one of the same bones that was most obviously missing from the skeletal remains you showed me out at the Johnson farm. I'm telling you, you need to talk to this guy."

"Oh yeah, I'm going to walk up to him and casually say, 'That's a fine looking finger-bone you got there, buddy. Where'd you get it?'"

"And you're the one with the P.I. license." She got up abruptly, walked up to the platform and said a few words to the kid while he was on an interlude break. When he jumped back in, she returned.

"You get a date with Charlie Chan?"

"Skip the shuck and listen O'Reilly. While I made a song request, I got a good look at a number of things. One, that tuning peg is pure skeletal of Homo sapiens, a proximal phalanx, the finger-bone closest to the knuckle. The same one missing from the bones you showed me at Johnson's. Two, his bow is also rather unique. Fiddle bows are strung with coarse Mongolian horse hair. His has human hair on it."

Pause. "You finally got my attention, Laura." I sat back, let out a long, low breath, and tried to think this one through.

A female in a black dress stood next to the kid now, in profile. I don't know where she came from. She had milk-white skin and long black hair and she began singing lead on "Crazy," swaying gently with the melody. She was no Patsy Cline, but she had a strong voice and a beauty about her. When she turned front, the other side of her face had a purple birth mark that covered her cheek. It didn't really detract from her beauty, but it was startling in its sudden contrast.

She stood at a crooked angle wearing only one shoe, because the other one was kicked off to the side with a broken heel. When the song went to instrumental, the kid put down his fiddle, took her in his arms and started dancing with her. Here they were, these two phantoms in black, twirling on stage, her trying to keep up while limping aimlessly in one shoe. It was a fruitless exercise in frustration, and she finally collapsed on the plywood decking and just sat there as "Crazy" played itself out to the end.

"What do we do, Laura?"

"Like I said, you're the one with the P.I. license."

"You don't seriously believe that bone could be linked to Vernon Johnson in any way, do you?"

"It's an opportunity I wouldn't pass up, but it's your case, O'Reilly."

"Betty Chalmers thought Vernon might have been coming out here or maybe to the Grange Hall to reminisce about old times and some young musician he saw a few years back. What interest would he have in someone like Charlie Chan?"

"Like I said, it's your show."

When I looked up, the woman was in the corner staring at us and the kid was gone. His fiddle was gone. Its case was gone. The band was breaking, so I went up to ask the bass player about the kid.

"Thrash? He took off. Didn't you hear that screeching sound?"

"No," I said. I guessed I was too deep in options with Laura to know what he was talking about. "You say his name is Thrash?"

"That's what he goes by. Every time he plays with us he sounds great, then all of a sudden all he can get is that screeching sound out of it. That's when he packs up and takes off."

"Where can I find him? He live around here?"

"No. Wichita somewhere. He plays guitar in a Grunge band, but he's so damn good on the fiddle, we let him fill in whenever Slim's not available for us. The guy loves it. Does it for free. Figure that. Grunge band but he loves playing for free with us."

"I need to talk to him. Ah… I want him to play a Bar-mitzvah I got coming up. You know where I can find him?"

The bass player looked at me strange-like. "Well, the Grunge band he's in is called Passing Gas. I think it's a take-off on that old Seattle group called Fartz. Plays every Friday night at some club on West Maple. Don't know the name of it."

"Thanks." I was out the door and into the parking lot, but the kid was nowhere to be seen.

Laura and I pulled off the crushed gravel and onto the packed dirt county road a few minutes later, and I noticed Phil leaning against his patrol car in the parking lot. I saw him in my rear-view as he grabbed a hold of his open door, eased himself down and into the car and followed us out. About a mile down the road I swung the pickup across the hardpan, got out and waited. A minute later, he rolled to a stop, pulled his body up out of the vehicle and advanced on me, but I spoke first.

"What the hell you doing following me, Phil?"

"What are you talking about?"

"This isn't the first time, is it? You got anything other than a standard issue 12 gauge in there?" I gestured toward the patrol car. "Say, maybe something high power with a scope? Something you could shoot at large rocks from a distance with?"

"I don't know what you're talking about, but I want to give you some advice." The night was cool, but standing in the beam of his headlights, I could see beads of perspiration on his forehead rolling down his cheeks and into the folds of flesh under his chin.

"You're putting your nose where it doesn't belong. You need to stick to your measly little skip trace jobs, things you can handle, and quit trying to complicate things that don't need complicating."

"You're hiding something, Phil." I took a step toward him. "Keep the hell away from me and quit trying to tell me-"

He interrupted me, thrusting a finger in my face. "Threatening an officer of the law will get you-"

"Oh, officer." Laura slid into the driver's side of the cab as well as into her cloyingly sweet vocal range. "Officer. Excuse my friend. He's had a little too much to drink and I'm driving him home."

"Who are you, lady?"

"I'm a friend of the friend. Jimmy, be a good boy, get in here now and let me get you back home safely. Friends don't let friends drive... well, you know, officer." She flapped her eyelashes at him.

The red heat in my forehead probably matched my hair color, but I backed away, got in and Laura slowly turned the pickup and headed off down the county road. I saw Phil out the back window, hands on hips, staring at us as we drove away.

When Laura and I got back to the bungalow, Janie was asleep on the couch and the ending song on the Long Black Veil CD was playing, "The Rocky Road to Dublin." Laura woke her up and we could tell she had been crying, with long streaks of tears that stained her cheeks.

"What's wrong, Janie?" I looked down on my reading table, saw an open volume of Seamus Heaney poems and two yellowed newspaper articles, brittle with age. She saw me notice them.

"I'm sorry, Mr. 'O.' I didn't mean to find those, they fell out of that book when I reached for a Yeats book and knocked that one over by mistake. It was an accident, honest."

"That's okay, Janie," I said. I picked up the clippings. I hadn't looked at them in a couple of years. One was an account of my wife's death. The other, her obituary. "Is this why you've been crying?"

She wiped a tear streak off her face. "Yes. I guess I knew you were married once, but I never knew what happened. I didn't know she was-" She broke off and couldn't say the word.

"Murdered," I said, finishing it for her, and Laura looked at me to see if I was alright. I still had trouble saying it myself.

"That's so terrible. I'm sorry, I just didn't know. I didn't mean to intrude or anything."

"It was a long time ago, Janie. Don't worry about it. You didn't do anything wrong. I picked up the two articles Janie had discovered, and looked at the obituary that began "O'Reilly, Sondra (Jameson), 42, Beloved wife of..." I put it on top of the article headlined "Two Killed At Convenience Store," and slipped them back in the Heaney book next to the opening poem, "The Rain Stick," where they'd been kept for the last five years. Sondra had never read the poem, but she'd loved the sound of a rain stick we had. She'd sit on the couch, tipping it back and forth, listening to its gentle, musical flow. I put the book back on the shelf.

"That Long Black Veil CD is great. You didn't tell me that Indian group played with Jagger and Morrison," Janie said.

I decided it was time to inform her, if not educate her a little. "Janie, they're Irish. The Chieftains, the Indian group, as you call them, is Irish."

"They got Indians in Ireland? I didn't know that."

I thought better about explaining it all to her and decided another time might be more suitable.

Laura and I drove her home in my truck. All the lights were out at her house, so Laura and I waited on the porch while Janie went in. She returned to tell us her mother's friend was gone. So was her mother.

"Call me if you have any trouble, Janie. Not just tonight. Anytime."

"I will Mr. 'O'. Thanks. By the way, can you come Saturday morning? It's our first softball game of the summer league at Two Rivers Fields down to Wichita. I'm pitching."

"I wouldn't miss it."

We both sat in silence driving the few blocks back to my place for Laura to get her red 'Vette, but I knew we were thinking the same thing. That a kid who had that much uncertainty and even potential harm in her life could be so solid, was a testimony to at least a degree of goodness and balance in the universe.

13

"Jack, has the coroner's report on Vernon Johnson come in yet?"

"Yes it has." Jack Sampson was the other deputy, the third man in Chisholm, and he looked down, a little guilty. "It came through on the fax late last night, but Phil said nobody can look at it. He's in charge, Alex being gone and all."

It was Friday morning and I had just hit the jackpot at our local blond brick halls of justice. Phil wasn't there and Jack was putty in my hands.

"Jack, let me lay the cards on the table," I said, being as trite as I could. "I can haul my butt down to the regional medical center in Wichita and file a request, or to the Sedgwick County Clerk's office and do the same, but you know as well as I do, this is a matter of public record. If I tell them it was denied to me up here, it's just going to come back to haunt you, and you'll have hell to pay. More problems than you want to deal with in a month of Sundays."

He thought about this for a moment, then went to the files and brought back the coroner's report on Vernon Johnson's death. "I guess it doesn't matter much one way or the other." He handed me the autopsy report, and I sat at Phil's desk reading it.

The sum of it was that there was blunt force trauma to the back of the skull that could not be accounted for by the position of the body in relation to the tractor accident, and the ligature marks on his neck had no explanation either. Death had occurred face down. There was no indication of coronary occlusion. My conclusion: There was plenty of suspicion to spread around. After I left the station, I stopped by the Johnson's house, and when LaVonda told me Bob was working, we talked for awhile, and then I went down to their hardware store on Commercial.

"Bob, anyone let you know the results of the autopsy?"

"No, Jimmy, they haven't give me nothing yet. You know something, anything at all?"

I was always amazed at the lack of communication between agencies. I tried to explain to Bob in a way that was gentle, yet let him know he was correct. There was evidence indicating someone had used physical force contributing to Vernon's death, I told him, and with what we knew about the bones, I would continue to pursue it until I found the truth. Then I asked another tough question, mainly just to see what Bob knew or didn't know.

"Bob, was Vernon seeing anyone that you know of?"

"What do you mean?"

"You know. Did he have a lady-friend, or anything like that?"

"You must be crazy, Jimmy. Dad was almost eighty. Lady-friend?"

"You're right, Bob. I don't know what I was thinking."

But as I was walking out the door, he said, "You know, Jimmy, Dad did say a few weeks ago if I called in the evening and he wasn't home, to try another number he gave me. That didn't make no sense to me at the time, but, well, you don't think-"

"No, I wouldn't give it a second thought, Bob."

I thanked him for his time, reassured him that I would continue my efforts, and walked the few blocks to Doc Smally's office and climbed the stairs. The door was locked and the note still posted next to it. On the way home, I drove by Smally's house on the south side of town. No car. Shades all drawn. No one answered the door. No evidence of any human activity. Doc Smally's whereabouts was still unknown.

Laura had been a beat cop like me, became a homicide detective in Chicago, earned a PhD becoming an authority on bones, was a marksman and Aikido Dan, and attained a sense of fashion somewhere along the way that defied what I knew about her in her earlier incarnation. But one thing about her never changed. Her outrage at the helplessness of victims and her passion to help them and to correct the social evils that perpetrated their conditions.

Once, back as a part of the gang-of-five, she watched as a cop hit a bag lady with his nightstick. He struck a woman who was living in a cardboard box in December in McAdams Park. Laura told the cop she was going to report him, which she did after getting his name and badge number, and then brought the woman back to her apartment, much to the chagrin of her roommate, until she could arrange for shelter for her through social services.

So it was no surprise to me that the first thing Friday morning, while I talked Jack Sampson into letting me read Vernon's autopsy report, she walked into SRS in a red silk two-piece suit, matching high-heels and a contrasting charcoal scarf, and filed a report on the home situation of one Janie Clayton, with the possible charges of child abandonment against the mother.

The complications this act brought about were a ways down the road, but the immediate effect was that an SRS case worker showed up at my door that afternoon, asking questions, which I dutifully answered. Then the case worker arrived at the Clayton house to find Janie home alone with no idea as to what was happening or why. Everything seemed normal and A-Okay to her. Why was this strange woman asking these questions? But Laura was not one to let matters rest, and this one would have to play itself out.

After the SRS worker left, I did set repetitions on my weights and then five minutes on a heavy standing bag and five minutes on a speed bag. I had boxed in college and then was a cruiserweight on the police team. I didn't get in the ring anymore, except for an occasional sparing session. When I finished, I ran one of my four mile section runs. One mile west, one north, one east, and one south, a perfect square, a measured and platted section. While I clocked myself in quarter mile increments and checked my heart rate, combines arrived and readied themselves to start thwacking their way through fields, harvesting grain, and all the while I planned my foray into the back alleys of Wichita. My quest for the only connection I had to Vernon's possible murder, a farfetched phalanx connection. My quest for Thrash.

14

"I'm looking for Thrash."
"Dude?"
"Thrash? Where's Thrash?" I said it louder, thinking that volume might help communication.
The emaciated gentleman with snake tattoos curling out of his tank top and down and around each arm evidently didn't understand what I said. He was setting up a trap set on the bandstand inside a club called In-Heat on West Maple in Wichita, and he was having trouble inserting tab A into slot B.
"Thrash? The dude's a no-show."
"What do you mean?"
"That fucker supposed to be here an hour ago to set up. I called three times on my cell. No answer, man."
I questioned whether he had the ability to actually operate a cell phone. "Where can I find him?" I asked.
"Dude?"
"You know where he lives?" I shouted it out.

"South Wabash, man." And he spit out an address. "You see him, tell him I'm gonna shove this snare stand up his ass."

I looked around at the pre-crowd empty interior of the cobbled-together structure where odors of stale smoke and old vomit mingled. A bartender was doing set-up at his well. In one corner padded mats hung on the walls for the mosh-pit crowd. It looked like where the high school wrestling team might set up to practice if they were in a Friday the Thirteenth movie.

"What's his real name?"

"Dude?"

I yelled, "What's Thrash's real name?" I felt my vocal cords starting to go.

"His real name? Thrash. The dude's name is Thrash. You just asked me about him. Something wrong with you?"

"Thank you. You've been most helpful," I said as I started to exit.

"Dude?"

My guess was I wasn't going to get the last word in, so I didn't respond.

I walked out the front door which was propped open with a plastic chair. A soiled, torn flyer was scotched taped to the door proclaiming that Passing Gas played on Friday night and a group called Nails in Your Groin on Saturday. I wondered if it shouldn't be the other way around, with the one event, perhaps leading to the other. A sort of cause and effect, if you will.

The weather report had indicated two approaching fronts and a collision between them scheduled for late afternoon. The stuff of typical June weather in Kansas. The stuff tornado chasers love. Outside, the temperature had dropped fifteen or twenty degrees in the short time I was in In-Heat. A complete darkness descended from the black clouds that moved in, and my face stung with dust that pelted it in the wind. I got in my truck and headed toward Wabash, but the Tornado sirens went off and a few minutes later the rain hit.

It came with the wind in driving sheets, rocking my pickup, and obliterating my view. I pulled under an overpass to wait it out and listened to the deafening sound, like being in a fifty gallon drum with someone beating on it with sledge hammers in each hand. A good twenty minutes passed before the rain let up enough that I could see. I pulled out from the safety of the overpass and headed for Wabash, the rain keeping a steady beat on my cab as I drove.

It was an old two-story wood frame in a section where houses were sandwiched in-between single story industrial buildings. It had been quartered, two apartments below and two above. The address drummer-boy provided was one of the halves, one of the above ones. No lights were on anywhere, and a rickety, open-face stairway canted straight up to the second floor and Thrash's place.

The rain had reduced itself to a steady drizzle, and that, along with the dilapidated condition of the stairs made it slow going, but at the top I paused and then knocked. No answer. I turned the knob and an unlocked door gave way and opened in.

"Thrash? You here?" I shouted through the partially opened door. "Your band wants to know if you're showing up for your gig." Still, no answer. I swung the door full-open and peered into the dark. My hand fumbled on the wall and flicked a switch.

Other than a mattress on the floor and two used syringes next to it, various drug related objects, some clothes, toiletries and a few personal items, there wasn't much there. No Thrash or his fiddle or its case.

I eased my way back down the exterior stairs and drove downtown. It was time to enlist some help. It was late, but I gave it a shot. I passed through security at City Hall and got authorization to go up to sixth floor homicide to meet with Charlie Daniels.

"Lorna Doone, O'Reilly, what are you doing here?" she said, when I walked in. I'd forgotten that old expression she used whenever she was amazed by something. "Lorna Doone." She just shook her head while staring at me.

I'd worked a beat with Charlie, Charlotte Daniels, twenty years ago and we'd made a good team. After I left WPD and set up my P.I. shingle, I relied on her for help and contacts. She got me out of more than one scrape. She'd never use anything like a throw-down, but she'd muddied the waters on at least one occasion and it kept me from taking a fall.

When I had decided to go find the person who murdered my wife after the police failed to do so, my blind rage caused me to pistol-whip the man whom I was sure had done it, and I nearly killed him. It turned out not to be him. But because the man was wanted for several home invasions which included two rapes and a number of brutal beatings, Charlie was able to get the right people to look the other way. She saved my newly acquired P.I. license, as well as probably keeping me from doing some time myself. It also made me second-guess my conclusions on more than one occasion. But we hadn't had much contact in the years that I'd just been doing skip trace work.

"What's happening, Bruiser?" Bruiser was a reference to my boxing days as a cruiserweight. Cruiser the Bruiser they called me. "When are you going to come up and see me sometime, O'Reilly?" she asked.

A year after my wife died, Charlie called and asked me to come by. She always used the old Mae West movie line about coming up and seeing her sometime. Her intention was clear, no doubt about it, but I put her off. She was sturdy and handsome, not undesirable, but I wasn't ready and when she kept calling and I kept denying her, she finally gave up. Here she was, asking again.

"I'm not here to flirt, Charlie. I've got business to discuss."

She got red-faced and looked away. "Okay, what do you need this time?"

"Look Charlie, I need your help. I got what I think is a probable homicide of a man named Vernon Johnson up in Chisholm, and the local Keystone Cops not only classify it as a natural cause, but it looks like they're covering something up. The coroner's report backs me up, too."

"What does that have to do with anything down here?"

"The only guy I can possibly connect to it all has a Wichita address, but when I went by the place it was pretty-well stripped. Nobody and no effects of anybody staying there permanently, other than some drug paraphernalia. He's a musician and I'm looking for him, for his fiddle and for the case he keeps it in. Anything you can do for me would help."

"What's his name?"

I looked away and took a deep breath. "Thrash."

"You got to be kidding."

"That's all I got, Charlie. He plays in a Grunge band and that's what he goes by. Thrash."

"Your probable homicide is outside my jurisdiction."

"Charlie? Please?"

"I'll see what I can find out for you, but you'll have to rethink your stance on coming up to see me sometime."

I winked at her. "Always a possibility, Charlie. Always"

As I walked out, I looked back through the office window and watched her type up a statement she'd been working on. She pecked with two fingers on her computer keyboard, eyes staring straight at the keys, and there was a beauty about her intensity, and earnestness in how she attacked the chore, and an innocence that belied all the gruesome details of her daily routine of death. She had a flush in her cheeks. I could not honestly say why I'd never called her.

    Late that night, or maybe it was early the next morning, I walked out of City Hall, exhausted and beat, and drove to East Douglas. Bomber had several rental properties as a sideline, and one was a brownstone near East High School on Douglas. There was a one room walkup in the rear of the complex he could never rent, at least to anyone he could trust, so he gave me the key for whenever I was working a skip trace and needed to stay in the city. It had a stand-alone shower, toilet, and bed. No kitchen except for a hotplate. That's where I crashed for the night.

15

GET Your nOSe OUT of OthER peepLS BISniS OR ELse.

The note, a strange mixture of lower-case and capital letters with misspellings and all, was unsigned, crudely folded and stuck in my storm door. I found it when I returned home Saturday afternoon.

I sat down on the steps staring at the bizarre note wondering what was going on or if Phil had some goon trying to scare me off my investigation. Buford Thomas also came to mind.

The day had been a good one up until that point. The morning had been baby-blue, and tender. Little wisps of cotton floated on the breeze, drifting over from the cottonwood trees by the lakes adjoining the county park when, earlier, I had arrived at Two Rivers sports complex. I parked next to Laura's red 'Vette. The air was sweet and cool in the lungs and made me feel like I just drank fresh well-water. Other than small branches and leaves on the ground and puddles of water scattered about, there was no hint of the violence that swept through with the torrential rains the night before. Distant crowd noise from the game, the sounds of "batter, batter" being called out, gave a peacefulness to the day.

I climbed the aluminum bleachers and sat next to Laura. Janie was walking out to the pitcher's plate for the start of the fourth inning, and she waved when she saw me in the stands. Laura and I watched the game and did not talk of bones or death or Vernon or abandoned children, and between games of the doubleheader we met Janie in the parking lot where a pink trailer sold Heavenly Snow. We took our cups of shaved ice back to the stands and talked and laughed and joked as we enjoyed the exotic flavored syrup they'd been drenched in. It was Janie's treat. She used money I'd paid her for house sitting to buy us snow cones.

"How does a skinny kid like you have such a powerful pitch?" I asked Janie.

"I don't know. Last year when I went from slow-pitch to fast-pitch, it just seemed to come natural. But I work at it a lot, too."

Laura smiled at her. Janie just smiled back, proud of herself. She'd pitched a two hit shutout and her team won, 5-0.

"I have to get ready for the second game. They're switching me to left field. Thanks Mr. 'O,' and you too, Laura, for coming today. I really appreciate it. It means a lot, especially since my mom can't make it."

We thanked her for the treat. She smiled again and raced down the bleachers and on to the field.

The day seemed so true and flawless and so far away from the ugliness of the city and its drug sub-culture, it made me feel there really was some sort of perfection in this world. I tried to hold onto that feeling for as long as I could, but by the third inning of the second game I finally began telling Laura what I'd found on Wabash, and that Thrash and his fiddle were dead-ends.

Her cell phone rang. "Yours or mine?"

"I still don't pack a cell, Laura. I never have and I never will. You know that. I hate them."

"I was sure you would have emerged from the dark ages by now. I swear, you're a card carrying Luddite, O'Reilly."

Her conversation indicated a rendezvous arrangement. "Do you still keep a string of those young ones in your stable?" I asked.

She smiled, and then switched her attention back to the game. Amongst the gang-of-five, Laura was the one who played the field, and her proclivities had not changed over the years.

After the game, another win, we saw Janie off on the team van, and I started back to Chisholm, seeing the true results, the reality of last night's storm. Combines sat dead in the muddy fields. The wheat harvest had come to a halt.

But now I sat on my front porch, puzzling at this strange note demanding that I get my nose out of other peoples' business, humorous in some ways, but ominous in others. I was startled by a loud horn honking. I looked up and the Mobley Mobile station's red tow truck was in front of my house, Allen Mobley at the wheel.

Allen, the owner's son, is a high school senior for the coming school year, the starting quarterback for the hometown Titan's, and he has already received three letters requesting permission for college coaches to come visit him and his parents on their recruiting trips. He's also gotten one academic scholarship offer. The girls go wild over his dark hair and handsome angular face. He climbed down off the high running board and walked up to my porch.

"Mr. O'Reilly, there was some weird guy at the station today asking questions about you. I figured I better let you know, especially with you looking into Mr. Johnson's death and all."

"Who was he, Allen?"

"I never saw him before. He drove a beat-up old pickup painted with a rust-colored primer. Tall guy, big barrel chest and a thick neck like a wrestler."

"What was weird about him?"

"I don't know. He was just strange. Besides, he had bib-overalls on with creases and work boots that creaked when he walked, and I saw bags of Farmland fertilizer in his truck bed sticking out from under a tarp. But the weird thing is he says to me, 'Boy, can you point me to where Jimmy O'Reilly's office is?' When I told him you don't do private eye work anymore and don't have an office, he says, 'Oh, I'm in insurance and I need to see him about a policy that's lapsed.' But he wasn't dressed like any insurance man I've ever seen."

"You sure you've never seen him before?"

"Yes, sir, and here's another strange thing. He only wanted five dollars worth and when he started asking all these questions, I said, 'You from around here?' He says, 'Oh, just up the road apiece.' But I took my time, squeegeed his window and then wiped some mud off of his license plate. He claimed he's from around here, but he had a Rice County tag. I just got a bad feeling about him, if you know what I mean."

"Thanks Allen. I appreciate you letting me know."

He started to walk back to the truck, and then turned to me again. "One other thing, Mr. O'Reilly, and I feel bad about this. When he asked where you lived I told him here on the west side of town at the corner of Sixth and Grant. I'm sorry. He kind of caught me off my guard."

"Thanks, Allen. Don't you worry about it."

I looked at the hand-scrawled note again and then folded it back up. Now there were three possibilities. Phil, Buford and a large man from Rice County. Inside, I filed the note, and then decided it might be a good time to cash in on my interpretation of an implied invitation to revisit Buford. An invitation I couldn't pass up.

Buford's faded black truck sat parked outside the pool hall as I drove through town, serving as an even stronger invitation. His Rottweilers stood and began their snarling routine as soon as I turned in his drive. They strained at their chains and segued from snarl to full-throated bark when I walked up and onto the porch. But I stopped short. Out beyond the dogs, where the bones had been, all that remained was an empty space. The bones had been cleared away leaving a round spot of barren earth. On the porch, the front door was locked, but I'd grabbed my B and E kit and had it open in seconds.

The inside of the house was no better off than the outside, with the added attraction of a foul odor that smelled like a backed-up drainpipe. Junk was stacked so high everywhere, I doubted I could find anything, even if I knew what to look for. He had an open gun rack with several shotguns and three scoped rifles. Hmmm. That gave me pause, considering the shot I'd taken to the stone. He had a knife case with umpteen knives with blades ranging from a few inches to more than a foot, and printed instructions on how to set up equipment to siphon irrigation water off of ponds and other bodies of water. That squared with what Bob had talked about.

Here was a man who had unrestricted access to Vernon's adjoining property and who was illegally taking water. Did he come and go for other reasons? Did bones exchange locations, and if so, why? Whose bones were they? He had scoped rifles. Did he fire the round at me outside the spring house? Of course, that person drove off down the county road. He didn't just slip back over a property line through a field.

I moved into the dining room and found some notes he'd written about the siphoning procedure. The hand writing didn't look anything like the threatening note I'd received, but then that was probably disguised intentionally. More stacks of clutter were scattered everywhere. On one small table, programs had been piled up about a foot high. They were performance programs like the ones Betty gave to Vernon. Some from Missouri, some from around here. On top of the stack lay a picture postcard with a photo of the Grand Ole Opry. Great. Another music lover.

That's when I sensed his presence. I turned slowly, and down the hall toward the bedroom, a Rottweiler sat staring patiently at me. He knew I'd been there the entire time and simply watched and lay in wait for me. I had a mental flashback. You didn't count, dummy. There had been only three chained dogs when I drove up. Fido here, is number four.

Fido rose slowly and silently from his predatory crouch, and then began with a low growl. He had a massive jaw that could probably manage a good sized jackrabbit in one crunch. I felt the weight of the blue lapis in my pocket and wondered if Fido would consider a turtle sacrifice. Probably not.

"Good doggie. Such a well-behaved puppy." I spoke softly, inching my way along the dining room table. He wasn't impressed. One leap brought him to the end of the hall, saliva already dripping from his mouth at the thought of me as a hors d'oeuvre.

Mid-second leap I spotted the plate of crumbled brownies on the table. I flung them to the floor and Fido came to a screeching halt, dropped on his haunches and started snarfing them up. I didn't wait to ask him if they were moist enough. I was out the door and in my truck in a millisecond.

I was exhausted. I poured myself a glass of red and made an early evening of it, but before I could climb into bed, Bob called.

"Jimmy, you been gone and I didn't know if you got the news. Dad's funeral's set for Monday morning. It's graveside, and mostly just family, but we would like you to be there if you can."

"I certainly will be there, Bob. And, thank you."

"I got a question for you Jimmy. When word got out about the arrangements, Betty Chalmers called and asked permission to attend. I told her no, and she seemed real upset. Do you know anything about this?"

There was an awkward silence as I struggled for the right words. "Bob, sometimes parents keep things from their children. Even grown children. Who knows why? Vernon and Betty had become quite close of late, and, well… maybe you might want to reconsider Betty's request."

16

I keep a bass boat out at Cheney Reservoir for serious angling, but when I just want to fish as a means to think things through, I head to a farm owned by a friend of mine named Wiley. He's got a five acre stocked pond full of flathead catfish, and I have an open invitation to throw in a line whenever I want. So Sunday morning I rose early, while the church crowd still slept soundly in their beds, put my rod, tackle box, lawn chair and my one gallon tub of SureShot catfish punch bait in the bed of my truck and drove out to Wiley's place.

Out west of Chisholm I passed more half-harvested fields with combines sitting idle. It was another morning of cloudless blue sky and light air, and the wind coming through my open truck window carried the sweet, moist scent of partially cut wheat. I drove with one hand on the wheel and the other hanging out the window. I passed a chicken hawk sitting on a fencepost scanning the terrain for a possible meal, and heard bobwhites calling each other.

I parked along a dirt road on the north side of Wiley's property a quarter of a mile from a hedgerow, spread open and crawled through two strands of barbed wire, then toted my gear out to the spillway of his pond. I always use a fourteen pound test line with a number two treble hook and a one ounce slipping egg sinker. I put my bobber in a set position between the first and second rod guides, and then I did the dirty. I opened the tub of punch bait, a mixture of cheese and blood and other disgusting unknown items, put my hook into it and used a paint stir stick to punch the hook down into it, then pulled up the glob of magic. You don't want to touch it, because the stink's so bad flies won't even come near it and it takes a week to wash off your hands. I once touched it accidentally, and no one would come near me for two weeks.

I took the lapis turtle out of my pocket, set it on the tackle box, and then cast out off the spillway and sat down on my lawn chair to think. It didn't matter whether I caught anything or not. I had to address the week's events and come to some kind of conclusion as to what I was involved in. I stared at the stone turtle, then out at the still bobber in the murky pond water, then back at the turtle again.

My great-great grandparents, Mark and Bridget O'Reilly emigrated from Cork, Ireland in the 1800s to escape the killing and torture of their kinsmen by the British landed gentry living in the Big Houses. They made their way to the now defunct town of Runnymede in Harper County, Kansas. Mark O'Reilly was probably lured there by cheap land advertised by the railroad. All you had to do was "prove it up," said the railroad posters. But Mark O'Reilly wound up making a good living by teaching the sons of English noblemen how to farm and ranch, the sons of the very ones who were oppressing his own relatives back in his native Ireland.

But, when the parents of these English dandies found out they were playing polo and partying instead of ranching, they pulled the plug on funding. So, with the source of his income gone, my great-great grandfather wound up in Lawrence, Kansas about the time Quantrill's Raiders massacred one hundred and fifty men in the town, and he found himself fighting for the Freestaters and abolitionists against the pro-slavery forces, and enmeshed in the Kansas-Missouri boarder wars.

Violence has followed the O'Reilly clan wherever they went. I put an end to it after my wife was killed. I divorced myself from it, left the WPD and worked as a P.I. for awhile, but that wound up with just as much brutality involved. So, ultimately, I took on the bill-paying, mundane work of skip tracing. But if there is such a thing as ancestral memory, maybe I'm hardwired for this stuff. Maybe I can't escape it, because here I was, back in the thick of it all, immersed in killings and drugs and not even knowing how it all happened.

I thought back through the week's events and tried to sort them out and make some sense of it all. In one week's time I had managed to threaten an officer of the law, get shot at, be threatened by that same police officer, be threatened in a bizarre note on my doorstep by a person or persons unknown, commit a B and E offense, take on the investigation of what might be the murder of Vernon Johnson, and be party to what could be considered obstruction of justice with the bones of another possible homicide. Oh yes, and for good measure, I had allowed a friend to drag me into an official SRS investigation of possible child abuse.

Not bad for one week's work. My O'Reilly ancestors should be proud of me. If I had any hope of sorting all this out, I needed to prioritize what must be dealt with and then get to it.

One, Thrash and his fiddle seemed to be a dead-end for the present, yet I knew I would have to use my connections and re-enter the drug scene to find out what I could. Two, I had no way to pursue the unknown man with fertilizer who apparently left the threatening note, at least not at this point. Three, I needed to talk with Doctor Joseph Smally, but he was mysteriously unavailable. But four, it seemed to me if there was a possible connection between Vernon's death and the bones gone missing, me being shot at, and the reciprocal threats between Phil and me, then Phil would be a good place to start.

Out in the pond a snapping turtle's head broke the water's surface and looked around as if mocking my lack of success. The flatheads weren't biting, but that didn't matter. I'd gotten what I came after.

As I packed up my gear there was a flash of light from off in the distance. I looked at the hedgerow of Osage Orange trees and saw the flash again, like sun on car metal, except there was no road beyond the hedgerow and no machinery was operating in the wet fields. Then again, it was also like sun off of binocular lenses.

I grabbed my binoculars and saw a figure beyond the hedgerow closing the door on a large, black SUV with smoked glass windows. It turned north at the end of the trees and disappeared in a puff of road dust. Whoever it was, vanished into the dust.

17

I walked in on Deputy Phil Turffe unannounced. He wasn't pleased to see me.

"Thought we'd have a sit-down over the Vernon Johnson investigation," I said.

"There is no investigation." He closed a file drawer where he'd just placed some papers.

"How can that be after what the autopsy report laid out."

He waddled over to a desk and wheezed as he sat down hard in an oak captain's chair. "One, you had no cause to go and get Bob Johnson to have his father cut open like that. Two, you had no right to look at that report."

"One, if you have that much concern for the Johnsons, you would be conducting an actual investigation instead of what looks to me to be a cover-up. Two, I have every right to look. It's public record and you know it."

"Then file the proper papers to see them." He was getting red in the face now. "And I'm going to tell you something else. Keep your nose out of this investigation or I'm going to bring you up on obstruction of justice charges."

"So there is an investigation. Do you acknowledge there are enough questions to investigate this as a possible homicide?"

"I didn't say that." He looked down for a second, then said, "We're looking into a few things, that's all."

"Has Doc Smally contacted you lately?"

"Why would I hear from him?"

"You're blowing out your ass again, Phil, just like a sea turtle. Now let me tell you something. This is the second time you've told me to keep my nose out of things. My nose. Did you have anything to do with the threatening note on my door that told me to keep my nose out, or else? Did you have anything to do with me being shot at out at the Johnson place? If you did, I'll have some charges of my own for you." My neck muscles were forming a knotted cord again.

"I don't know nothing about none of those things." He looked confused and disoriented. "If someone is threatening you, file a report," he said.

"What did you do with the bones, Phil?"

There was a flicker in his eyes and he looked away, even more flustered. "What the hell you talking about? Bones? You've gone off the deep end, Jimmy. I've got to get out on patrol now. Leave me alone."

He rose to go, but his eyes gave him away. He knew all right. I followed him out the back door pelting him with more questions as he fitted his campaign hat on while walking toward the patrol car.

"Have you been able to determine anything about Vernon's whereabouts from the time he left Latte Dottie's the day before he was found? Why was he still wearing the same clothes? What caused the blunt force trauma injury to his head? Why does your report say he died face up when all the physical evidence says face down? What's the time lag between actual time of death to when he was found? Was his body moved from some other place to where he was found? What happened to the footprints? Where are the bones?"

He ignored me as he lowered himself into his patrol car, then he rolled his car window up and drove off down the alley. Way to go O'Reilly. You not only didn't find anything out, you managed to piss the guy off even more. That's not true, I thought. I did find out he knows something about the bones. His eyes gave that much away.

I walked around the corner and climbed the stairs to Doc Smally's office. The note proclaiming a family emergency was still taped next to the door.

On my way back home I swung by Janie's house with the single intention of talking to her mother about the SRS report that Laura filed.

Francine Clayton had led a hard life. She woke up one morning twelve years ago to find a note from her husband consisting of three words: "Goodbye. So sorry." The car was gone and bank account closed out, and she never heard from him again. She had a two year old daughter and had never worked a day in her life. She waitressed for a few years, but wound up drinking away her tips and wages in the local taverns, and that's where she met most of the men she took up with. She had no means of transportation because she couldn't save enough for a down-payment on a car. With no visible means of support, she seemed to use the men she found for whatever resources they could provide for as long as they could provide them, whether it meant going away for a period of time with one of them, or bringing one home and giving him roaming privileges in the yard and bedroom, like taking in a stray dog.

Francine sat in a lawn chair on her front porch smoking a cigarette as I pulled up to the curb. As soon as she saw me, she rose to go into the house, but she didn't move quickly and I was out with a greeting before she could get to the door.

"Hello, Francine."

Her eyes held that indecision of whether to go on in the house, pretending she hadn't heard me, or stay. She stopped and faced me but didn't speak.

Francine was sad looking. Her body had taken on a heaviness over the years and she no longer possessed the physical allure she once had. The chain smoking showed in her lined face and she spoke with a slow, gravelly smoker's voice, punctuated by coughs. Her eyes were vacant and lackluster, and gray specks flecked her once shiny blond hair. I thought I detected a bruise on her right cheek bone hidden under heavy makeup. Barefoot, she was dressed in dirty jeans and a ribbed white shell that pooched out over her belly. She looked much older than a woman in her mid-thirties.

She sat back down, holding a cigarette that had at least an inch of ash on it, but made no attempt to knock it off into her ashtray. Her eyes were nervous and kept darting back toward the house.

I tried for a cheerful start. "I saw Janie win the first game of her doubleheader on Saturday," I said.

She looked away, and I could see the guilt in her eyes because she wasn't there herself.

"Is that so?" She coughed her dry smoker's cough, then said, still looking away, "I don't get to too many of them myself, things being what they are and all."

Oh boy, great start O'Reilly. I put my foot on the first step and started up the porch, but she flinched and pulled back in her chair as if she expected someone was about to strike her, so I stopped and leaned against the weather-beaten newel post.

"Well, maybe later in the season," I said. "There's lots more games." After a pause where she kept looking off with her vacant stare, I continued. "A friend of mine was concerned about Janie and she spoke with a Social Services representative."

"I know about that. They came around. I don't much appreciate that, Mr. O'Reilly, somebody I don't know intruding on me and my girl's life."

"Our concern is that she might be exposed to some, well, some unsavory individuals."

"Unsavory? What's that mean?"

"I don't want to be unkind, but some of the people who have been here at the house-"

"I can take care of my own, Mr. O'Reilly, and as for who's here in my house, that's none of your business. Your friend is stirring up trouble, but I got friends of my own and we all look after one another when it counts." Touché. Felt about an inch small. Her cigarette ash fell off and onto her jeans. She glanced at the house again and I saw a man's hand part the window curtain slightly. Then she put out the stub and lit another one.

"There are other times when no one is here at all. That can be a dangerous situation for a young girl, alone and by herself." I said.

"I have to go away sometimes. Places I can't take Janie." Then she got a scared look in her face and stood up. She looked directly at me for the first time. "They ain't going to take my Janie away from me, are they, Mr. O'Reilly?"

"I don't know Francine, but you could help the situation yourself you know, just by what you do."

"I try to do good. I come outside to smoke now instead of making what they call that second-hand stuff inside."

I saw tears in her eyes, but when she turned and went in the house, the look of fear and the countenance of a person who had been beaten by life was what stayed with me. As I walked back out to my truck, I glanced up her drive and saw a rust-colored pickup in the detached garage in back of her house. I went the length of the drive and looked. The tag was from Rice County. When I climbed the porch steps and pounded on the door, nobody answered.

    I drove home with a sadness of my own, wondering how some people came to the weariness which defined their lives and circumscribed their own mean worlds. The Francines on this earth stood as a mystery, and it all made precious little sense to me. But something Francine said stayed with me. She had said something about taking care of her own and how friends look after one another when it counts.

    Doc Smally had no family left and was alone in the world now, but I remembered he did have a lifelong friend, another old doctor in Wichita who he used to go on hunting trips with. Weisenberger. Doctor something-or-other Weisenberger. It stuck with me because the name had a humorous sound to it. I wondered if an old friend might be taking care of his own, when it counts.

    I found only one Weisenburger listed in the Wichita directory. Dr. Solomon Weisenberger (ret.). He answered on the seventh ring by simply saying "Yes?"

    I didn't introduce myself. I just launched right into it. "I'd like to speak with Joseph Smally, please," I said.

    There was a long silence, then, "You must have dialed the wrong number."

    "Is this the residence of Doctor Solomon Weisenberger?"

    "Yes, it is, but I don't practice anymore, I'm-"

    "Then I have the right number, and I believe Joseph Smally might be-"

    "No. I don't know anyone by that name."

    He hung up and the line went dead.

    I jotted down the address listed in the directory.

18

Taps is a mournful song anytime it is played. Much more so when played by a lone bugler at a funeral. The brassy lament with its long, pure notes rose up high on the morning breezes and carried out across the cemetery and over the wheat fields at the south end of town.

Vernon's casket sat on the mechanical lift over his open grave, draped in both an American flag and a U. S. Marine Corp flag. As the last strains of Taps trailed off, all I could hear was the faraway drone of combines in the fields. Two days of clear Kansas skies and sunshine worked their magic and the cutting resumed.

We stood around the grave site, Bob, Lavonda, their two sons and daughters-in-law who came in from out of town, and a younger brother of Vernon's who lived in Oklahoma. Then there was myself and Betty Chalmers. Besides the minister, the bugler and a rifleman, that was it. If there were any protesters that Alice mentioned, they hadn't bothered to show up. Oh, and then there was Tick.

Bob brought Tick along, and he sat on his haunches, staring straight ahead at the casket, as if at attention.

The smell of damp earth from the open grave mingled with a sweet odor from a nearby lilac bush in bloom, as if decay and life could be mixed together and coexist. I don't know, maybe they could. Life and death, coming and going. One and the same.

When I had arrived, LaVonda welcomed me and whispered, "I wished we'd a known about Betty. We had her over yesterday, after what you told Bob. I just wished we would a known."

"We're laying him to rest with his medals and decorations," Bob added, as if trying to justify the presence of the bugler and the rifleman.

The minister said a few words, no eulogy mind you, and then read a Bible verse. I think it was that famous one from Ecclesiastes. Betty came forward and laid an old phonograph record on the casket. "Lefty Frizzell," she said softly. "One of his favorites." The rifleman sent off twenty-one single reports echoing in the still morning, counter pointed by the metallic snap of chambering each round.

When Vernon's casket lowered into the grave, Tick rose, went to the edge of the opening, and stared down into it. Then he circled three times and lay next to it.

That was it. Nothing fancy. That was Vernon's tribute.

I went through the metal detectors on the first floor after checking my Ruger, and then I clocked in on the sixth floor of City Hall on Main in Wichita and went straight to Charlie's cubicle.

Her eyes lit up and her full, round face smiled when she saw me. "What are you doing here, O'Reilly?"

"That's the second time you asked me that in three days," I said. "I'm taking you up on your offer. I decided to come up and see you sometime." I winked.

"Hey, don't kid around with me. Besides, this wasn't exactly the venue I had in mind. You're just the person I wanted to see though. Nice timing. I'll tell you what, come with me and lunch is my treat."

Ten minutes later we slid into a booth at the Old Mill Tasty Shop over on Douglas. She ordered a burger, fries and chocolate malt, and when I asked for a salad with dressing on the side, she said, "Lorna Doone. Come on O'Reilly, order some grease. You need to bulk up."

"Thanks anyway, Charlie, but I'm trying to keep my girlish figure."

"You're too much, O'Reilly. Look, you know that Thrash guy you were looking for? We found him in the database. His actual name is John Phillips."

"As in 'Sousa'?"

"You got it. John Phillips, but hold the Sousa. I checked around and found out he's been on Narcotics' radar for a couple of years. We know he's a mule for somebody, and he's probably a user himself, but they can't get anything on him and he's always one step ahead of them."

"Looks like we have a mutual interest in Mr. Phillips, at least from Narcotics point of view." I pulled out the pictures I'd gotten developed, the ones I'd taken of the bones in Johnson's spring house cave, and explained what happened and about their disappearance. "I'm trying to establish a link. Vernon Johnson's obsession with these bones, his recent interest in investigating the local music scene, his mysterious last trip he made to who knows where, these all must have some connection to John Phillips, AKA Thrash, with his fiddle playing and his phalanx tuning peg."

"You might try keeping us informed about things and in a timely manner, O'Reilly. And I'm telling you up front, don't go looking for this guy, Thrash. You've been out of the business too long. These are nasty people and they'll eat you alive."

"I'll keep the advice in mind, Charlie," I said.

"I'm telling you, O'Reilly, leave it to us. We'll find him, and when we're done, you can have him for whatever you need. You got my word on it."

I knew she didn't believe me when I said I'd back away. Before I started my Thrash search, I drove by the address I wrote down for the good doctor, Weisenberger. It was a brick and wood combo ranch, built probably in the late fifties and hadn't been kept up too well.

A thin man, stooped at the shoulders, and with gray, curly hair opened the door when I knocked, and then tried to close it quickly when I introduced myself and referenced the previous day's phone call. My foot moved quicker than his hand.

"I need to see Joseph Smally," I said. "But I'm also worried about him. I would really appreciate the chance to talk with you."

His face took on a weary look, and he motioned me in to a dark, cluttered living room, where we sat.

"I'm worried about Doc Smally," I said. "I think he is in some kind of trouble, and I don't want to see anything happen to him."

He looked off and thought for a moment. "He's not here now. He was, but he's not anymore. After your call yesterday, he became afraid, packed his bag and left. I am worried, too. I'm not sure what he has done, but he is very frightened and I fear what might happen to him."

"Do you have any idea where he might have gone?"

"He didn't say." He thought for another moment. "There is a cabin where we used to stay on our hunting trips, west of Chisholm. I'll write the directions down for you. It is possible he went there. But you must promise me you will give him help if you find him."

"I will, and thank you Doctor. I'll let you know what I find out."

I started making the rounds of bars where musicians hang out. If Thrash was no longer staying at his residence on Wabash, he'd have to hook up with somebody to stay with, and other musicians seemed a likely route.

I'd been to six places with no success when I parked across the street from Zingers, a ramshackle, clapboard dive that was a haunt for both musicians and druggies. Two for the price of one. It was dusk, that in-between time when dark descended but light still glowed, and it looked like you were peering through a filter. Your eyes played tricks on you in this kind of light. I decided to sit back and observe the action in the parking lot before going in to look around.

Several individuals came and went, most of them looking around furtively before they entered the premises. Then I saw him. Charlie Chan. At least I thought it was him. There was still some light bouncing off car hoods and mingling with the dusk, and his face flashed back and forth in the hazy air when he walked out, talking on a cell phone, crossed the parking lot and leaned against a faded old gray four-door Buick Electra that looked like it was from the seventies. He hung up, folded his arms and waited.

A minute later a monstrous black Denali pulled up in front of him, like the one I'd seen out by Wiley's pond. Its smoked windows kept me from seeing the driver, but the driver's window powered down and a long, pale arm extended out and handed him a package. When he stepped up on the running board to take it, a face came out of the window to give him a kiss. It was that face of beauty with the birth mark on one side. The woman with one shoe.

Then she opened the door, climbed down and embraced Thrash, almost swallowing his skinny body with her arms, and her long black hair completely obscured his head while she kissed him long and passionately.

When she drove off, she stopped at the edge of the parking lot when Thrash called after her.

"Clare. You and me, Babe, forever. Right?"

"Sure, Thrash. You and me."

He started toward the Denali. "When you getting rid of Larry? That turd husband of yours is nothing but a pain."

But her window powered up and she was gone.

Decision time. Go after the woman called Clare in the SUV, or get Thrash? I should have called Charlie, but I didn't pack a cell phone and I didn't have change for a pay phone inside. That was a nice excuse, anyway. I started to follow Thrash into Zingers, unsure of what to say or how to approach him.

Instead, I walked over to the Electra first. I peered through the window and saw a fiddle case lying in the back seat. When I tried the back door it wasn't locked, so I looked around and then slid low into the back seat, keeping my head down. When I opened the case, there it was in front of me. The fiddle with the proximal phalanx for a tuning peg. It was dark and there weren't any overhead spots in the parking lot, so I took a pen light out of my pocket and turned the fiddle over looking at it closely under the beam. On the underside a signature was etched into the wood: ABonelli.

I was about to close up the case and pose some questions to Thrash when I acted out of pure impulse. I unscrewed the finger-bone tuning peg and slipped it into my pocket. I thought about looking at the bow when I heard voices, so I closed the case, slipped out of the door and duck-walked around a couple of cars, then stood up, slammed a car door as if I'd just gotten out and walked across the lot toward Zinger's entrance like I'd just arrived.

Thrash was exiting with the Denali package-delivery under his arm just as I got to the door. He might be muling for this Clare woman, but he must have taken a hit out of it, because he had every tell-tale sign a tweeker could exhibit. His red face flushed with sweat and his eyes glazed over with dilated pupils. He talked to himself so fast I could barely make out what he said.

"No shit, man. No kidding. I don't know what the hell was going on. They were coming after me and I was fighting them off, I think they were like aliens or something and were like trying to invade my body, like Revenge of the Body Snatchers or something or whatever that old Steve McQueen movie was and they wanted to take over my body and use it like a vessel…"

His speech was so rapid it was like vaudevillian patter and I half expected him to drop to the ground in a pratfall. But I didn't laugh because he saw me and his arms started flailing the air while he screamed in my face, "Pod. Alien pod, I'll kill you, man."

I side-stepped him, backed into the doorway and watched him stumble out to his Electra, get in and swirl his tires as he spun out of the lot.

I walked over to the bartender and said, "I need to make a phone call."

"There's a payphone next to the johns," he said.

I flashed my P.I. badge like it was a cop ID and said, "Official police business. Give me the bar phone."

He looked at me skeptically and put the phone in front of me, but stood close by listening while he dried rocks glasses with a dirty bar towel. I dialed 911.

"Listen good," I said, when the operator answered. "I'm at Zingers on the west side. I just witnessed a drug transaction, and one John Phillips, who is wanted as a material witness in a possible murder and who is a known drug dealer, just left the parking lot traveling west in a gray 1970s Buick Electra."

"Sir, please state your name and the location you are calling from."

I hung up and walked out the door with the bartender staring open-mouthed behind me, his towel stuck in a rocks glass.

19

    The town of Reed sits north and east of Chisholm in the same river lowlands, but directly on the Little Arkansas. Late the next morning I drove to Reed to find Antonio Bonelli. Through a phone call I made to an antique shop in Wichita that also specializes in violin repairs, I was told that the signature "Bonelli" on an instrument indicates it was made by Luigi Bonelli, an Italian immigrant who settled in Reed and became known for his finely crafted violins. His son, Antonio, learned the art, and when he took over, he expanded his repertoire to include guitars as well, but used the signature "ABonelli" to distinguish his work from his father's.
    It was another brilliant blue Kansas sky, and whatever coolness existed absorbed quickly in the late morning sun. It would be a scorcher by mid-afternoon, but the humidity was low, and on the county road to Reed, grain trucks, filled to the top with harvest, passed me as they rolled

along toward storage silos and elevators in the small towns scattered in the lowlands.

At the south edge of Reed a combine on one side of the road worked its way through a field half cut, and one on the other side was stopped, spewing its load into a waiting grain truck.

I had to cut over two blocks off the county road to get to the main drag in town, and then I remembered what today was. Red, white and blue lined the length of the main street, and every home and business displayed a flag as well. It was the funeral of one of Reed's own. A recent graduate of the high school, newly married with a child born while he served in Iraq, this native son whose name I could not remember, was being buried in the local cemetery. An Improvised Explosive Device killed him along a roadside north of Baghdad, and the entire town mourned him today with a memorial service at the Presbyterian Church and a graveside interment.

Closed signs adorned every establishment and no one walked the streets, so I drove back over to the county road and to the edge of town where its only convenience store was located. It was open for business, and inside, a lone teenage clerk sat behind the counter reading a comic book.

"I was wondering if you could give me some directions?" I asked.

He looked up from the comic book. "Where to?"

"I'm looking for Antonio Bonelli's shop, or maybe his home, since everything is closed today."

"One and the same," he said. "His home is his shop. Or his shop is his home. Whatever. It's over on State. Go three blocks up, turn left, and State is three bocks over. I forget the address, but he's got a sign in the yard."

"Thanks." When I walked out the door, he picked up a piece of bubble gum from the counter and began unwrapping it.

Bonelli's house was an old two-story Victorian kept in immaculate condition, with a wrap-around porch complete with scrolled gingerbread. From the look of it, he probably lived upstairs and used the first floor for sales and his workshop. A closed sign hung in the door window, but I went ahead and turned the key on the old brass ringer next to the door. Nobody answered, and it took five or six tries before I heard anyone stirring.

Finally, a figure descended the narrow stairs that ended in the vestibule just behind the front door. A hand pulled back the latch, partially opened the door, and I found myself looking at a man of about forty, short and with a slight build.

"I'm looking for Antonio Bonelli," I said.

"Tony. Tony Bonelli. That's me, but I'm closed today."

"I understand," I said. "My name is Jimmy O'Reilly. I'm a private investigator licensed by the State of Kansas, and I'm looking into what could be a murder. You may possibly be of some help."

"You must have the wrong person. I wouldn't know anything about a murder."

"I'd just like to ask you a couple of questions. It would only take a few minutes of your time, and it could help to resolve some questions surrounding a recent death in the area."

"I really don't-"

It didn't take much force. I had the door pushed open and stood in the entry way before he could object, and kept on walking through a front room where guitars, violins and other string instruments were on display, each with some odd distinguishing feature about it. There were guitars with bodies in all shapes and sizes including one built to look like flames and another with pieces of colored glass imbedded in it. Bridges on violins were constructed of odd objects and artifacts, and I saw tuning pegs of all kinds.

One looked like the tip of a bull's horn. He finally resigned himself to the situation and led me to a back workroom where instruments hung from the ceiling in various stages of construction, and there were two work chairs where we could sit.

"I can't help but notice, Mr. Bonelli," I said, after we sat, "that you seem to have a penchant for the bizarre in the instruments you construct." I looked at his hands. Like his build, they were slight and very delicate.

"It's sort of my trade mark, what distinguishes my work artistically, I guess. The trick is to craft an artistic creation that is unique, and yet retain all the pure qualities of sound and resonance. This violin, for instance," and he pointed to one hanging near us, "is an experiment in material variations. The violin's belly is always made of spruce, but I am using metals imbedded in its structure to see what happens to tonal quality."

"I see. Well my question relates to a fiddle you made, probably some years ago. Do you recall a fiddle you created with a proximal phalanx?"

"A what?"

"A finger bone. It had a skeletal finger bone for a tuning peg."

His eyes became unfocused and he looked away. "No. No, I...I have no recollection of anything like that."

"It bears your signature," I said.

"Perhaps someone altered it or-"

"It also has a bow with human hair for strings."

"Oh my, that is distressing." He still looked away, not meeting my eyes.

"You're a very poor liar, Mr. Bonelli. You also seem to be a meticulous person." I noticed his rows of file drawers along the wall. "I'm sure you've kept careful records over the years. They could be subpoenaed by the court if necessary, and you would be forced to testify in open court. That can sometimes be unpleasant."

He physically withdrew and started to hyperventilate, mumbling to himself. "I didn't do anything wrong, and now someone else has come."

"Someone else?"

He caught himself. "No. I just meant-"

"Who was here before me?"

I could see him thinking of how to lie, and then he changed his mind. "Another man, a couple of weeks ago. He asked the same questions you did and I told him about the bone and blond hair."

Blondie, I thought to myself. "What was the man's name?"

"I didn't ask. He was a tall, elderly man."

"That man was Vernon Johnson. He is now deceased. Possibly murdered." Bonelli recoiled and his eyes got bigger. "As to whether you did anything wrong, Mr. Bonelli, I couldn't say, but I need to know the details surrounding this incident."

He paused and thought for a moment, clutching the arms of his wood work chair, trying to regain an even breathing rhythm. Finally, he spoke. "It was several years ago and I was out searching for material to use. I'm always looking for something unique, something different to distinguish my work. I often walk to find natural objects to incorporate into my creations. I was walking along the Little Arkansas and saw these bones. I took a finger bone. I didn't think it would be missed. The skull still had hair attached, long blond hair, and I clipped some of that to use, too. I didn't mean any harm."

"I'm sure you didn't," I said. "Did you report this skeleton to the authorities?"

He looked away again, and I could see the fear in his eyes. "Not for awhile. I was afraid to. A couple of weeks later I went to our chief down at the police department, he was brand new on the job at the time, and told him about it. We went out to the riverbank together, and I showed him the spot, but we'd had heavy rains and some spring flooding, so there wasn't anything there. I guess it had all washed away. He just looked at me like I was crazy."

"Let me get this straight, Mr. Bonelli. You found a possible murder victim and didn't try to convince anyone of it?"

He started to stammer and hyperventilate again, but then he regained his breathing and found his voice. "Let me understand this correctly. You are not a police officer?"

"No, I'm not," I said.

"And you have no authority in this matter?" he asked.

"No, I do not."

"Then I think it is best you leave."

"Yes. Thank you. You've been most helpful," I said. "I'll let myself out. I'm sorry for the young man from your community who lost his life. Maybe someday all these deaths will have some resolution."

"You seem like an honest man, one who has no ax to grind, as they say. Are you?"

"I'd like to think so."

"Do you think I will be in trouble over all of this?"

"I have no idea, Mr. Bonelli." I started out and then turned back to him. "One more thing. Who did you sell this particular instrument to?"

"We have our spring music festival each year, you know." He paused and seemed to be thinking about it, or perhaps how to phrase what he was about to tell me. "There was some young woman who always came and played each year with the others. They played so well. I will never forget her. Beautiful. A milk white complexion and jet black hair, but with a birth mark on one side of her face. She fell in love with the instrument when she first saw it and purchased it on the spot."

"A woman by the name of Clare something-or-other, perhaps?"

"I don't know. I never asked her."

"You don't seem to be overly interested in names, Mr. Bonelli."

I left him staring at the finished creatures of his artistic sensibilities, and the half-made future instruments, animals of his efforts, dangling on strings all around him, like grotesque Mardi gras skeletons. And with the name of Clare running through my mind.

20

I drove back to Chisholm under blue skies, but in a blue funk of my own. Later, sitting on my terrace, staring at the cut wheat fields beyond, I sorted through what I just learned. The bones Vernon found most likely had been washed down the Little Arkansas when he discovered them on his place. The fiddle Bonelli made using one of those bones and the hair from its skeleton's skull was probably sold to the woman who danced with one shoe, Clare, and who drives the Denali. At least from what Bonelli said, if he was telling the truth. Did she give the fiddle to Thrash? Why would she do that if she'd fallen in love with it at first sight, as Bonelli said? How had Vernon traced whatever information he had to Tony Bonelli? What was the connection between Vernon's finding the bones and his death? I still couldn't make sense of anything.

I looked out past the terrace and saw Tiresias racing across the yard with amazing speed. Everyone thinks of turtles as slow and plodding creatures, but quite to the contrary, they are not only agile, but can have tremendous bursts of speed. He stopped short suddenly and picked a cricket out of the air that was in mid-jump, and began chewing it until its juices ran down the side of his mouth.

"How'd you do that Ty?" I called out to him. He looked in my direction with what had to be a smile of satisfaction. I have no idea how he sees with no sight.

It wasn't until I went back inside I even noticed evidence that Janie had been by. Everything was in its place. Neat and tidy. A hand-written note under a magnet on my refrigerator said I was low on Irish Cheddar and needed to pick some up from Piccadilly Market the next time I was in Wichita. Bless her soul, what would I do without her.

That was when I heard a scraping sound on my front door. By the time I pulled back the curtain, a large man was getting into a rust colored pickup. I opened the door and a folded scrap of paper fell off the screen door. As I picked it up I yelled at him but he was already speeding off. The paper was another crudely scrawled note: you haVNt Qwit YoUR Time iS Up.

If this was the guy who had been threatening me, I wasn't going to let him get away. I hopped in my truck and took after him. At Commercial I looked both ways and saw him two blocks north, driving toward the edge of town. I followed, but decided to stay back and see where he was going. After several minutes on the two-lane and a couple of turns, it was obvious we were headed toward Reed, and I wondered if he had some connection to Bonelli.

Was this menace also making the same contacts and asking the same questions I was? I was more perplexed now than ever. I couldn't tell if he'd picked me up in his rearview, but he kept a steady pace and I stayed well-back of him.

When he hit Reed he passed the turn to Bonelli's house, so that couldn't have been it, and then he went further north, turned right, and pulled up across the street from the Presbyterian Church. I could see a crowd gathered on the sidewalk, most of them carrying signs and placards, and shouting something at everyone entering the church for the funeral. The man I followed got out of his truck, took his tee-shirt off, and pulled another one on, down over his head and thick torso. Then he took two signs out of his truck bed and walked toward the crowd. Large red letters emblazoned on the back of his shirt read: GOD HATES FAGS. When he joined the crowd, he handed one of the signs to another member.

I parked a few cars back, and when I walked past his truck I jotted down his Rice County license number on the note he'd left at my screen door. When I was part way there, I was able to see some of the placards better. One read: GOD BLESS THE BOMBS KILLING OUR TROOPS. An elderly couple walking down the sidewalk, obviously dressed for the memorial, shook their heads and seemed quite distraught.

"What's going on at the church?" I asked.

"It's those damned people from Topeka that call themselves Baptists," the man answered. "They go around picketing soldiers' funerals."

These must be the protestors Alice had been worried about showing up at Vernon's funeral.

"Surely somebody can prevent this," I said.

They both just shook their heads again and walked on toward the crowd and the church. As I got closer I saw another sign that read: THANK GOD FOR IEDs, and another: THANK GOD FOR AIDS, and then the chants and shouts became more audible. At the moment they were shouting "Thank God for the mortar," over and over.

I crossed the street and approached the group. "What the hell you people think you're doing?" I shouted. Then, a large arm came across my chest, catching me from behind.

I swung around and a uniformed Reed city police officer said, "Back off buddy, step over here with me."

"You can't let these people do this," I said, and turned back toward the crowd. He stepped in front of me and put his nightstick across my chest with a fair amount of force.

"You so much as touch one of them, they will file a civil action against you and then use the proceeds to fund their hate activities. You're playing into their hands. It's just what these people hope you'll do."

All of a sudden they took up a new chant, and I heard "They turned America over to fags; they're coming home in body bags."

"What do these crackpots want?" I asked the officer.

"They think our soldiers are being killed as God's punishment for America tolerating homosexuality. Pretty twisted isn't it?"

"You got to be able to do something about this," I said.

"I know it's crazy, but they got First Amendment rights."

"Crazy? It's insane," I said. "Look, that guy right there." I pointed to the man I'd followed. "He threatened me. How about my rights?" I pulled out the note from my screen door and showed it. "Arrest him and protect my rights, officer."

He read the note and then said, "Where did this occur?"

"Down in Chisholm where I live. I followed him up here."

"I'm sorry, but you need to file a report with Alex or one of your officers down there, where they have jurisdiction."

"Hey." I yelled at the man who left the note as he came to the near end of the picket line, waving the paper at him. "What the hell you doing threatening me?"

"You the one? Get the hell outta Francine Clayton's life, asshole." He shouted back.

Francine Clayton? What the hell was he talking about? Then the images clicked. The rust-colored truck in Francine's garage. The hand on the curtain in her window. What was his connection to-? I started toward him but the stick came across my chest again, more forcibly than before.

"If you're too chickenshit to do anything," I said to the officer, " I'm going-" But before I took two steps, he grabbed me by one arm and another officer held me by my other arm, then they dragged me back and pushed me down into a squad car.

The next thing I knew I was sitting in one of two cells in the Reed city jail.

"You arresting me?" I asked the officer.

"Let's just say we're taking you out of circulation for awhile. Look mister, I sympathize with you. That crowd's a bunch of idiots. But that soldier's family has been briefed about the situation by the military. They understand they have to ignore it and go on with their grieving."

"Talk about rights. You think a person would have the right to grieve in peace," I said. "So, are you charging me, or what?"

"Just going to hold you for awhile. Let you cool down."

"Overnight?"

"That might be best," he said. "I'll lock your Ruger in the safe until morning." They had relieved me of it when we arrived at the station. "Ruger 101? You a revolver guy, huh? Don't most of the fellows in your line of work use automatics?"

"I like wheelguns," I said. They're fast, easy, reliable. Never failed me yet."

"Seems strange to me."

"Am I allowed a phone call?"

"Just a minute." He walked out of the cell area around the corner to where the desks were, all two of them, and returned. He handed me a cell phone through the bars and said," We're pretty informal around here, but keep it to one call."

"How do I use this thing?" I had a blank look on my face.

"What are you talking about?"

"I've never used one before. I got cell phobia," I said, looking around me with an intended double entendre.

"Oh, for Pete's sake. Uses a revolver. Can't operate a cell phone." He showed me how to use it, then walked away shaking his head. "Remember, one call."

I stared at the machine in my hand. Sweat broke out on my forehead and I felt a tightness in my chest. "Come on, Bruiser," I said to myself. "Think your way through this one." Slowly, I began following his directions and punched in Charlie's desk number, hoping she was there.

Two rings, then, "Detective Daniels," in a flat monotone.

"Charlie, it's me. O'Reilly."

"You coming up to see me?" Her voice suddenly lost its flatness and became bright.

"I'm a little indisposed at the moment," I said, and explained the situation.

"Jesus, O'Reilly. You don't expect me to bail you out of this, do you?"

"Bail?" I took her literally. "No. They're just giving me lodging for the night. They'll kick me out in the morning, unless I do something stupid tonight," I said. "But I got a favor to ask. That guy I told you about that's been leaving me notes. Can you find out who he is? I think maybe he's up to no good. Maybe even tied in to this whole thing with Thrash, I mean the Phillips guy. I don't know." I gave her the license number off his truck.

"Yeah, sure, but you'll owe me big time. You may have to come up and see me to repay this debt." Then she imitated Brando's voice from 'The Godfather.' "I may call

113

upon you for a service someday." Then she dropped the imitation and said, "By the way, O'Reilly, you haven't been pretexting by any chance, have you?"

"Moi? Pretexting? That's illegal. Why do you ask?"

"There's a voice on a 911 tape called in from a place called Zingers that sounds suspiciously akin to yours. When I questioned the bartender, he said someone flashed what looked like a cop ID to use the phone."

"You stumped me on this one, Charlie. It's a mystery. Did you get him? Thrash?"

"No. He was long gone. Well, keep your nose clean, and check in with me on anything you got on Thrash."

"Will do. Oh, one other thing. You remember Laura Bascome?"

"Sure."

"Give her a call and tell her my situation. Tell her I got information I need to give her on some bones."

"Bones? You jumping Laura Bascome's bones? That's disappointing. What about me, O'Reilly?"

"They're standing in line, Babe. Take a number." I gave her Laura's phone number and hung up.

21

The next morning when I walked out, blinking, into bright sunshine with my reclaimed Ruger in my pocket holster, Laura's red Corvette sat diagonally in a parallel parking spot in front of the Reed city jail with a parking ticket on the windshield. She was nowhere in sight. The streets were empty and a silence belied the violence of yesterday's intrusion into humanity.

"Hey handsome, buy a girl a cup of coffee?"

I swung around and Laura, resplendent in mauve and teal silks, materialized out of nowhere and stood with one hip splayed out, her auburn hair reflecting the morning sun. I half expected her to swirl around and hit me with an Aikido kick.

"Ah," I said. "Me, a knight in distress and you, a damsel to the rescue."

"Don't flatter yourself. The dyke called and said you had some bones for sale. I presume they're not yours."

"One, Charlie's no dyke," I said.

"Oh, are you sweet on the lady? I'm jealous."

"Two," I said, "The bone, singular, is a gift to you." I pulled the proximal phalanx from my pocket and twirled it in-between my forefinger and thumb, taunting her. "Come back to my place and I'll show you my etchings."

We headed back to my bungalow, with her following my pickup in the red 'Vette, gunning the engine to let me know she resented being trapped behind me. The morning sun was already baking, and even though it was still June, its heat was more like July's intensity, but I pulled off to the side, got out and walked back to the 'Vette when she pulled off, too.

"What now, O'Reilly?"

"I want to make a detour," I said. "The coffee will have to wait."

She followed me for about a half an hour while I took a couple of wrong turns on back roads looking for the cabin Weisenberger gave me directions to. I finally found it on the edge of a giant wheat field that had small groves of trees and brush at various points in and around it. They would make for excellent cover for game birds. A great place for the seasonal hunts in fall and winter.

"You got a wonderful sense of direction, O'Reilly. Think you could have put a few more unnecessary turns in that little excursion?" Laura needled me as we walked toward the cabin, a small two-room, wood-frame with wide clapboards, painted a dark red. A hunter's special. I filled her in on Doc Smally as we walked the trail from where we'd parked the cars, next to two other vehicles.

"I'm telling you, you need to get the hell out of here and you need to do it now."

"But I don't know where to go. I haven't got any place else to run to."

"It doesn't matter where. Just pack the damn suitcase and let's go."

Doctors Weisenberger and Smally were arguing inside as Laura and I stood listening outside the cabin door.

"Don't waste anymore time, Joe. You don't know what these people might do to you if they find you. They may be desperate by now."

I started to knock, decided against it and opened the door. Smally sat on the bed next to an open suitcase, partially packed, with more clothes strewn about. Weisenberger stood next to him. They both fell silent and stared at us, until Weisenberger finally said, "I was afraid something like this might happen."

"Something like what, Doctor?" I asked. Laura and I stood opposite them and the small room felt crowded. "This is... an associate of mine, Laura Bascome. Laura, Doctors Solomon Weisenberger and Joseph Smally." They both stared at Laura.

"As soon as you left, I regretted telling you about this place." Weisenburger leaned over, closed the suitcase on what clothes were in it, picked it up and said, "Come, Joseph. We are leaving now." Smally stood, his tall and sturdy frame a counterpoint to Weisenberger's diminutive stature, and they started to walk out.

I stood in the door blocking their exit.

"You will let us pass now, Mr. O'Reilly." Weisenberger stood in front of me, his face practically in my chest.

"I can't do that. We have to talk."

Even together, the two of them with their elderly bodies were no match for me and they knew it. They retreated a couple of steps and fell silent, and then both sat on the side of the bed. I sat in a straight-backed wood chair opposite them, Laura standing next to me.

"Doc," I said. "I've known you for too many years to count, so this is a hard question to put to you. Did you have complicity in covering up the manner in which Vernon Johnson died?"

He hung his head and I could see how much this cost him.

"I'm so ashamed," he said. Vernon was a life-long patient and a friend. I'm so ashamed."

Laura put a hand on my shoulder. "Tell me what happened, Doc," I said.

"She came to me, a year or so ago. She talked me into it. I knew it was wrong, but you have to understand how bad off I was. I'm old and my patients are old and dying off and the new clinic in town gets the patients now and I owed a great deal of money. That's it. Money. I did it for the money, and she talked me into it. But still, I knew it was wrong from the beginning."

"Who is this she you are talking about?" I asked.

"I don't know her actual name but I wrote the prescriptions in the name of Carley Masters."

"You're not making a whole lot of sense, Doc. Money. Prescriptions. What are you talking about?" I knew where he was going, but I wanted him to sort it out in his mind and verbalize it. Weisenberger stepped in and began clarifying it all.

"I didn't know myself, although I suspected, until I came here today and we talked. Joe has been prescribing drugs for an individual who does not need them."

"When she came to me she asked for large amounts of antihistamines, allergy drugs with pseudoephedrine," Smally continued. "Old over the counter stuff that was no longer OTC since the state law changed. I knew why she wanted them. Others had come and asked, too."

"Meth?" I asked.

"Sure. They cook meth with them."

"But why the cover-up with Vernon?" I asked.

"She told me if I didn't say his death was natural causes, she would expose what I had been doing for the last year. I'd lose my license. My whole life would be ruined."

"So, Deputy Turffe forced you to sign the false death certificate?"

"Phil? No, he was there when I went to Watson's, but I don't recall he said as much. I just followed her instructions."

"What did this woman look like?" I asked.

"Young and pretty. Dark hair. She had this birth mark on one side of her face, but she was very pretty."

"Do you have any idea where she lives?" I asked.

"No. Like I said, I don't even know her real name." He thought for another moment and then said, "Come to think of it though, she came in once or twice with this young guy. Younger than her, I mean, and really scruffy looking. She'd tell him to meet her back at the place. That's what she called it. The place. And he'd ask which way he was supposed to take. I could tell from what she said it was north."

"North of town?"

"Yes, and he'd ask 'back roads or main way?' And by what she said I knew it was on a dirt road and I could tell their place was right on the Little Arkansas."

"Thank you, Doc. We're going to leave the two of you now."

"You mean," said Weisenberger, "you're not running us in, as they say?"

"No, I'm not 'running you in' as you put it. But listen to me, and listen well. Doc, you need to go to the authorities and tell them what you have just told me. Tell them everything."

"I know," he said. "I know I need to." There was shame in his voice.

"But," I said. "Don't go to Phil Turffe. There is too much danger in that. He may be complicit in all of this himself."

"Phil? I don't think so."

"Trust me, Doc. Go with your friend here. Go back to Wichita and see someone in Narcotics at WPD. Here is my card. Give it to them and tell them I sent you. Tell them your story. Promise me you will do this."

He stared at my card in his hand as if it represented some magical solution to his problem. "I will," he said.

We left them, sitting on the edge of the bed, two aging dinosaurs who looked as if the new order of species had redesigned the food chain and left them to their own ultimate extinction.

I fixed coffee for Laura, according to her request, and we set aside the flippancy, sat down in my reading area and got down to business.

"Can you tell anything from this?" I handed her the finger bone and told her where it came from and how I obtained it.

While she examined the phalanx, I called Charlie to check in on the license plate number for the leaver of harassing notes. While we talked, I unconsciously took the lapis turtle out, turned it over a couple of times, set it down with the others and then picked up a mottled bloodstone turtle and slipped it in my pocket. I don't think I even realized what I'd done at the time.

When I hung up, truly amazed at what Charlie told me, I explained the whole story to Laura.

"Here's the deal," I said. "This guy has left me two threatening notes. He was observed by Allen at the Mobile station behaving strangely, and he is involved in the Topeka group that pickets soldiers' funerals claiming God's divine wrath on America in retaliation for its own perversion. His name is Jerry Clawson. Now get this. Charlie says he is a registered sex offender, convicted of abusing males and females anywhere from five to fifteen years of age. But it doesn't end there. He hasn't been at his registered address for over one year and nobody knows where he currently resides, or his whereabouts."

She stared at the finger bone. "I'm betting you've got some qualms and you're second guessing the fact you took on this case for Bob Johnson."

"Qualms I got, but I can't go second guessing myself now. What I need are some answers. I've been threatened every step of the way on this, sometimes by this Clawson person, sometimes by Buford Thomas, sometimes by Phil, maybe somebody else even, I don't know. But then this Clawson guy, out of nowhere, says 'Get the hell outta Francine Clayton's life." I left off the explicative he used. "What does this religious nut of a sex offender's threats have to do with bones and Thrash, and most of all, Francine Clayton? And if anything, with Vernon Johnson? What's the connection here?"

"We got Clawson. We talked with Smally, and we got Phil. But what about this Bonelli guy you talked about? I don't get how he figures in all of this." She said.

"There's something about that character that bothers me. The whole setup. His shop, his explanations, his evasiveness. Something's wrong."

"You think he knows more than he's telling?"

"I'm about to make my third trip to Reed in two days. Care to join me?"

"Only if it's as exciting as my last visit."

"Park illegally again and you might get to spend a night in the clink."

She reached for her keys.

"Unh-unh. I'm not taking any chances. We're going in my truck."

22

"You didn't play square with me, Buddy."

Bonelli whipped around on his work stool, saw Laura first and then me, standing in the midst of his hanging artistic creations.

"You'll have to excuse us. We let ourselves in."

He looked at my Ruger, which I'd intentionally worn on an outside-the-shirt shoulder holster and there was fear in his eyes, but it turned to abject terror when I pulled a stool up next to him, close enough to breathe hard on him.

"What do you mean, I didn't play square?"

"I mean, you're holding out. I want to know everything."

"I told you everything. Everything I know."

"It doesn't quite add up, Bonelli. You mentioned the new police chief you talked to about it, but if I recall correctly, your chief here in Reed has been on the job as long as Alex down in Chisholm. He wouldn't have been new at the time."

"Well, I must have been confused about that. I-"

"That, and a few other details. You found the bones alright, but you didn't report it to any of the authorities did you?"

He started to hyperventilate, like the last time I interviewed him. Laura circled around behind me, eyeing him and looking at the hanging instruments. He looked back and forth at the two of us, gasping his short heavy breaths.

"Calm down, Bonelli." I moved in even closer and could smell his sour breath. "You said every year at the festival they played so well. Who played so well?"

"The woman who bought the violin."

"They. You said 'they.' Who else did you mean?"

"I said 'they?' I must have meant that in a general way. You know-"

Laura moved slowly down the line of instruments, her hand lightly touching each one just enough to send it knocking ever-so-slightly against the next one."

"Don't do that," he said.

In my mind, I suddenly saw the images of the programs from Buford's, and then the box of programs that Betty gave Vernon. Names clicked from when I'd gone through them.

"You figured it out, didn't you? You found the skeleton on the river, took the finger bone and hair, and then figured it out. Only you didn't go to the authorities, you went to her. Is that how it happened?"

"I don't know anything. I just-"

Laura made a quick, sudden move. She whirled around, her mauve silk slacks rippling gently as she turned, and did an Aikido kick above her waist and over the work counter, sending a bent piece of rosewood that was drying in clamps across the room and splintering against the wall. Bonelli expelled air with an incoherent word attached and raised half up. I clamped my hand on his bony shoulder and shoved him back down. He felt as light as the wood that just splintered and I was afraid I might crush him.

"Tell us how it happened," I said.

"No. There is nothing to tell."

Ever so slowly, Laura raised her right leg, high up, above her shoulder, balancing herself on her left leg. Her foot gently touched the bottom of a delicately crafted violin that bounced as she flexed her toes against it. Bonelli gasped again.

"The destruction of beauty ought to be a crime against humanity, don't you think, Bonelli? Maybe they could add it to the Geneva Convention rules. It would be a shame to lose objects as precious as these."

Laura, still holding her pose, flexed the foot harder and the violin jumped sharply and thudded against a heavy guitar hanging next to it, an echo resonating across the room.

"You're right. I figured it out," he shouted. "I figured it all out. Stop. Don't do that, please don't do that."

Laura lowered her leg, I stood, and we both faced him.

"Were they sisters?" I asked, thinking back to the programs again.

"Yes. Sisters."

"And the sisters are the 'they' you were talking about? The sisters used to play the music festivals here, together. Right?"

"Yes. I found the skeleton on the river, just as you said and I figured it out. Don't ask me how. I just knew. The one called Clare murdered her sister, Lael. It was Lael's skeleton I found."

Again, the programs. "Clare and Lael McCabe. The Singing McCabe Sisters. Is that her name? Clare McCabe?"

"She's married now. I don't know what it is now."

Laura and I exchanged a look, and then she spoke for the first time. "I'm guessing they lived upstream from you."

"Yes. When I went to her, she denied it at first, but I told her I had a finger bone and hair. She said nothing could be proved by that and I said no, but questions would be asked and she'd have a hard time explaining."

"So, you used that to extort money from her?" I said.

He hung his head, but didn't say anything.

"How much?"

He looked up and gestured with one hand to all of his instruments. "Enough for all of this. It was a dream I had to be able to create on this scale. But I gave her something for value, I most certainly did that. She got the fiddle with the bone tuning peg and the hair."

"How good of you," I said. "So, that's the real reason you didn't want anyone in here looking at your records. No accounting for the money, huh?" He nodded. "And over the years you've just kept milking her for more and adding to it all."

"Oh, no," he said. "Just the one time. We had an agreement."

"An agreement?" Laura said.

"Yes. Just the one payment. I would never think of breaking an agreement."

"Why not?"

"It would be ungentlemanly. I'm a gentleman, you know."

"Yeah," said Laura. "I could tell. I always admire that quality in a guy." She shook her head in disbelief, then looked around. "You sure do good work, Bonelli."

Back in my truck, I said, "You do good work yourself. Nice moves, Laura."

"Speaking of moves, where do we go from here?"

"Well, at least, we now know to whom the bones belong." I said.

"Kind of like, for whom the bell tolls?"

I smiled. "It tolls for Clare. The murderess. The question is, did she murder more than once? Did she murder Vernon Johnson, too?"

"I reiterate. Where do we go from here?"

"We go nowhere until we check on Janie. Remember, she may be in the same house with a convicted child molester."

We drove back to Chisholm in silence, and then sat in my truck outside the Clayton residence, which was closed up, locked and with no evidence of anyone present.

"I have a class to teach," she said. "You need to call Charlie and coordinate how to deal with this Clare woman. I'll call after my class about checking up and keeping tabs on Janie."

23

I sat staring at the phone. To call or not to call, that is the question. Whether 'tis nobler in the heart to suffer the slings of Charlie's outrageous...

Smally said north of town on the river. Bonelli gave us general directions. The images meshed. I took out the blondie paper with the lines on the other side and there it was. It was not a math class graphing exercise. It was a map and the intersecting lines showed roads north of Chisholm and the squiggly line was the river. Vernon found the way and now I had a clear route to Clare McCabe's whatever-her-last-name-is, place.

Phone. To call or not to call.

I had another problem. Janie and her sometimes-good, sometimes-not-so-good mother and Francine's sex offender of a boyfriend. Where was Janie? Besides my map to Clare's, I had an address from Charlie for Jerry Crawford's registered residence as a sex offender. Even if he hadn't been there in over a year.

To call or not to call. Sorry Charlie, it was a no-brainer.

"Good afternoon, Mam," I said to a woman weeding next to a detached garage.

"Howdy." She continued with her project, not looking up.

The address I had obtained from Charlie for Clawson's official address as a registered sex offender was in Sterling, Kansas, a town of about two thousand residents in Rice County.

"I'm looking for a man named Jerry Clawson. I was told this is, or at least it was, his residence."

"And who might you be?" She still did not look up at me.

"My name is Jimmy O'Reilly. I'm a private investigator looking into some matters for a client." I handed her one of my cards which she looked at as she finally stood up. The cadence of a tennis ball pinging against the other side of the garage filled the silence as she read the card.

On the other side of the structure, a boy of eight or nine practiced fielding groundballs by throwing a tennis ball against the wall, positioning himself for the bounce and catching them in his glove. His mother unpinned wash from a clothesline and put it in a basket.

"I be his sister," she said. She wore jeans with dirt crusted on the knees, and a blue work shirt, and her hair was tied back and up with a red kerchief. She took off her leather work gloves and thought for a moment while we listened to the kid's ball, and then said, "I don't know what your purpose is Mister, but I don't know his whereabouts, neither. If I did, I'd tell you, 'cause that worthless piece of shit's done nothin' but cause me grief. I only took him in when he got out of the clink 'cause he's family. Family ought to look out for each other, don't you think?"

"Have you seen or heard from him at all recently?" I asked.

"No I haven't and I don't want to. Oh, he comes and he goes. A week ago I come home and a fifty dollar bill that I always keep extra in my chiffarobe, and what he knows about, was gone. I never saw him, but I know it was him what took it."

"Do you have any idea where he might be staying?"

"Not the slightest idea at all."

"I know where Jerry's at." The pinging had stopped and the boy stood at the corner of the garage. We all stared at him. His mother stopped folding a sheet, mid-fold, and stared too.

We were all afraid to ask, but I ventured the question. "You know where Mr. Clawson is?"

"Jerry? Yeah, I know where Jerry is."

The boy's mother came over and said, "No you don't. You come in the house now. It's almost time for lunch."

I was not about to let this opportunity get away. I knelt down next to him and looked him in the eye. "Where? Where is it that you know Jerry is?"

"Oh, you know, that place where all the birds are. Out by where our school takes us on field trips to see the birds," he said. "He took me there once, 'cause I told him I like birds, and he has lots of candy he keeps there and he gave me some."

But the boy's mother yanked his arm and sped him off toward the house. I called after her, but she ignored me and shot through the back door with him. I looked at Clawson's sister and said, "You need to talk with that woman, and you need to talk to the authorities, too."

She hung her head in a grim countenance and slowly nodded agreement. Then she said, "That place he's speakin' of out by Quivera? That's my ex's old place. He's another piece of shit I never want to see again. Men."

"You're ex-husband lives there?" I asked.

"No. Nobody lives there. It was his parents' till they both passed. Then it set empty. It was so run down, didn't nobody want it. I didn't even know it was still standin'."

The place Jerry's sister referred to was on a dirt road just across the county line from Reno into Rice County. The Quivera National Wildlife Refuge bordered it on one side and nothing else was within miles of the house. Her directions contained very little specificity. Once I found the dirt road, it took two passes before I spotted a tilted mailbox with the faded letters on it she'd described. Even then, I wasn't sure, with the entrance so overgrown and obscuring the structures, until I got to the end of the long drive and saw the rundown house.

I parked between the barn and the house. When I got out, a muted stillness hovered over the place and I stood in an eerie silence looking around. A flock of Canada Geese flew overhead on their way to the wildlife refuge. I fingered my Ruger, now in a concealed under-the-shirt shoulder strap, wondering what I did if I ran into this possibly kidnapping, sexually perverted recidivist who might carry weapons of his own on him?

No vehicles present. Good news in terms of a confrontation. Bad news for locating Janie.

I walked up on the porch and peered through windows. I tried the door, which was unlocked, so I went in slow and cautious. There was a bedroom with a dirty mattress on the floor, and I covered my nose from the odor. In the kitchen there was a bowl of candy and an open box of Cheerios on the kitchen table, a few of them scattered on the floor. Somebody had eaten here recently. There was a wet, empty ice bag in the kitchen sink along with some empty two liter pop containers.

On the porch, I sat and took the stone turtle out of my pocket and set it on my knee, startled that it was the bloodstone, not the lapis. I'd forgotten I'd switched them out. Bloodstone for courage. For facing death. Turtles know things we don't know. They fly at midnight and see beyond the dark. The ancient Chinese used their shells to see the future. Just like Tiresias. He can...

I looked over at an open pole barn. Something wasn't right. There were stacks and stacks of supplies on a farm that was completely fallow. Nothing was in use here. What were the supplies for? I walked over, looked in, and there stood hundreds of sacks of fertilizer. Alan Mobley had said he noticed Farmland sacks in the truck, but here were literally thousands of them. Holy Shit. OKC redux.

Jerry Clawson. Sexual pervert. Homophobic. And now, possible homegrown terrorist. But no Janie.

Lights blazed in my bungalow and Laura's red 'Vette sat in my drive.

"What're you doing here?" I asked.

Laura sat on my couch as Janie walked out from the bathroom and they both looked at me as if I came from another planet.

"I've been worried sick about you, Janie. Where have you been?"

"Softball practice," she said simply, and I hit my hand to forehead. I hadn't even thought to check out the practice fields.

Laura eyed me and then said, "Francine is nowhere to be found. Janie's not sure what's happened to her, so I'm taking her home to stay with me tonight." She paused. "You call Charlie?"

"Yeah, sure."

"You lousy liar. Get your act together, O'Reilly. Call her and let me know what the score is. Then we'll decide what to do about all of our situations."

I made the call, but it wasn't to Charlie. It was to the KBI informing them of my find at Clawson's place.

That night, as I lay in my bed contemplating the roller coaster ride of the day, the forces of nature conspired. A mass of warm, moist air moving up from the Gulf of Mexico collided with cool, dry air descending out of Canada, in typical June Kansas fashion, and the unstable product spawned multiple funnel clouds on the High Plains. The event was well-anticipated, and The Weather Channel and CNN sent crews and correspondents to western Kansas where they set up shop, broadcasting live updates showing the intensity of rain, threatening clouds, the actual formation of wall clouds and their evolution into tornados, and home-made videos submitted by local storm spotters of tornados swooping down out of the sky and cutting wide swaths of destruction across the land.

A Weather Channel presenter stood in a yellow windbreaker, as if that could shield her from the environment, and reported live, shouting at the camera about the debris which sailed through the air and pelted her as she stood in the storm's path. She winced and grimaced into the camera, altering her stance as she tried to remain upright.

Tornado-chasers, a curious phenomenon recent to the culture, poured in from neighboring states and massed at critical points, based on what they were told by forecasters. They idled in vans with video cameras mounted on vehicles or in hand and at the ready, and cruised down back roads scanning the skies for any signs of wall and shelf clouds, and then went racing toward one with reckless abandon as soon as a sighting occurred. When a funnel descended, the chase began, and scores of vans instantly changed direction, looking for the road that would parallel the tornado's path.

None of this hysteria reached the Central Plains. Instead, in Chisholm, the sky roiled itself into cumulus clouds, towering fifty-thousand-foot thunderheads, and cloud-to-ground lightning fried transmitters and substations. The entire town was without electricity, and I lay in the dark in my underwear, on top of the sheets, sweating next to an open window where there was no movement of air to offer any relief from stifling heat and humidity.

I fell in and out of sleep, in my waking moments thinking of Janie and Clawson and Clare, and in my sleep, dreaming the nightmare I'd been free of for such a long time now. It came back upon me in a flash of copper, like a cottonmouth coiled on a river bank, striking, recoiling, and striking again, its poison seeping into veins and racing with blood to invade my body.

The progression of events never altered in the dream. The images were always the same: I pace the floor in our home in Wichita, just west of College Hill, re-check my watch, my wife gone too long for the walk to the corner convenience store on a cigarette run; my slow walk under old elms to the corner to check, expecting to meet her on her return, puffing one of the Virginia Slims she counts and doles out to herself on a measured basis; an empty street with no meeting; my arrival at the convenience store; the three cruisers; flashing lights; taken inside and shown for verification; the two bodies in the beer cooler laying face down; blood pooled in the clogged drain; got it execution style in the back of the head.

I awoke, as I'd always done, sitting upright, cold and shivering, with night-sweats and dizzy, my breathing shallow and labored, my heart pounding in my chest. I grabbed my jade turtle I kept on the nightstand for comfort. My mouth felt dry, my tongue swollen, and I couldn't swallow. I went to the bathroom sink and held my head under a faucet of cold, running water.

I looked out the window into the dark. A jag of lightning cut the sky, and in a flicker of light I saw Tiresias beneath the glass pane. His yellow striations glowed in the lightning pulses and he stared with his clouded eyes at the window.

Back in bed, propped up against pillows on my headboard, I took the small breeze that stirred now, offering itself through the open window, and tried to regain my breathing. I wondered what evil would descend upon me this time.

As was often the case, after the reoccurring dream, my grandfather's story would play over in my mind. James O'Reilly was a shanachie, a story-teller versed in the old Irish myths and tales, who received the stories handed down generation after generation and passed them on to others. This tale was the one about a famous Irish warrior named Oisin, and it always came to me after the nightmare.

In my grandfather's version, Oisin met a beautiful woman named Niamh in the forest, who promised to take him to Tir na nOg, the Land of Eternal Youth, where they would live and love happily forever. But Oisin eventually missed the real world, and when he returned for a brief visit, he was warned by Niamh not to dismount from the magic horse she gave him, or he would never be allowed to come back to her. Unfortunately, he stopped to help a poor farmer move a boulder, which he was able to do from his horse, but the saddle slipped, and when he fell to the ground he turned into an old man. Having lost his true love forever, he saw his homeland as a changed place, one of bleakness and full of sad people.

Finally, just before I fell asleep, the smell came to me, as it always did after the nightmare. The night my wife was killed, she leaned over and kissed me just before she walked out the door, her hair brushing across my face. Perfumed hair the color of ripe wheat. It held the fragrance of pine needles, a smell that always comforted me.

I fell into a deep pine-scented sleep, while thunder rumbled and lightning split the sky and Tiresias stood his watch. Neither the rains nor the tornados made it to the Central Plains.

24

The reading of Vernon Johnson's will was scheduled for the morning, and I had been asked to be there, although for the life of me, I couldn't figure out why. I planned on attending and then immediately setting out to find the place on Vernon's map where Clare lives. First, I stopped at the dry goods store to pick up several pair of socks to replace my toeless few I was down to.

"On your way to the will reading?" Alice asked as she wrapped up my purchase.

"Why, yes I am, Alice. How'd you know that?"

"Oh, a little birdie told me," she said in her quavering voice. She had a smug look on her face, and then she couldn't contain herself any longer. "What do you think Betty will do once she's rich?"

"Rich? Gibson guitars are worth quite a bit of money, Alice," I said, referring to the knowledge I had from my interview with Betty, "but I don't think inheriting one is going to make anybody rich."

"Oh, I wasn't talking about the guitar," she said, "I meant-" Then she saw the look on my face. "Oops."

"Another 'oops,' Alice? What's this one about?"

"Oh, nothing, nothing at all." And she toddled through the curtained door into the stockroom before I could get anymore out of her.

Outside, Buford Thomas spotted me on the street, took giant strides walking wildly with his arms swinging, and was in my face before I could get in my truck.

"We've got to stop meeting like this, Buford." I said. "People are starting to talk."

He seethed anger and had an irrational look in his eyes. "Somebody's been in my house."

"You ought to invest in a good security system. It'll pay for itself twice over."

"I know it was you and you're going to pay for it." He eyed a tire iron lying in the bed of my truck, but before his hand reached it, I came down hard with my right forearm, whacking his elbow on the lip of the bed. I gave him a left uppercut on his way down, and then he dropped to his knees, howling in pain. I picked up the socks off the pavement and tossed them in the cab and drove off down Commercial, trying to shake the sting out of my right arm, with Buford still on his knees.

"You have each been asked to be present because you have some interest at stake in the late Vernon Johnson's estate."

Ryan Blakely, like Doc Smally, was part of the old guard of Chisholm, and like the doctor, his law offices were up above other businesses and on the second story in an old building on Commercial. And just as there was the newer medical clinic in the south part of town, there was also a newer, younger law firm there, too. But Vernon had stayed loyal to the old lions of law, just as he had with his doctor.

"What I must ask each of you to do is remain respectful of Vernon's decisions and the rights of the others present, no matter what you think or believe you might be entitled to," Ryan said.

We all looked at each other, wondering a bit at his last statement, and of course, I had just been 'oopsed' by Alice, which heightened the curiosity even more for me. I sat in the middle of a semi-circle in front of Ryan Blakely's desk, with Bob and LaVonda on one side of me and Betty Chalmers on the other, and an empty seat on the end next to her. Ryan was about to continue when the door opened and his secretary ushered in an African-American gentleman none of us had ever seen before.

"I am sorry I'm late, Mr. Blakely." He walked to Ryan's desk and held out his hand. "I am Sammy Jones, Jr."

As they shook hands and then as Sammy Jones took the empty seat, the rest of us stared in complete bewilderment at this distinguished looking man in his fifties, dressed in a tailored suit. We all exchanged looks and then settled back into our chairs.

Once Ryan dispensed with the preliminaries, he announced an insurance policy disbursement to Vernon's two grandsons who were not present for the reading, and then the first surprise was mine.

"Jimmy, Vernon has bequeathed to you the following property, to wit: one baseball."

"A baseball? Vernon left me a baseball?"

"Bear with me, Jimmy. One baseball, signed by Greg Maddux, and thought to be the only known, authenticated ball from his only no-hitter ever thrown to this date."

"Excuse me," said Sammy Jones. "I feel like an intruder, not being from here, but I do know a little about baseball, and Greg Maddux has never thrown a no-hitter."

"Actually," I said, "he has. He threw a six-inning no-hitter for the Dodgers that was halted by rain, but he didn't officially get credit for it in the books, because he didn't go the whole nine innings. But how the hell did Vernon come by this?" I asked.

It was my turn to be stared at now, but the genius and generosity of Vernon was apparent to me. He had given me a memento from one of the greatest two-seam fastball pitchers ever, a tribute to me and to Vernon's own mentoring of me many years ago in a game we both loved dearly.

"Betty," Ryan continued, "Vernon has left you his 1934 Nick Lucas flattop Gibson guitar, which I believe you are already well-acquainted with, with the following instructions. 'Play this instrument every evening for the pleasure and pureness of the notes as well as for the memories it holds of us.'"

There were tears in Betty's eyes, but there was also a smile on her face. However, this still did not provide an answer to Alice's 'oops.'

"And now for you, Mr. Jones. Vernon Johnson has most generously endowed a full professor's chair in the name of Sampson Cleveland Jones at Washburn University's School of Law in Topeka."

We all stared at the man with absolutely no idea what this was about.

"That is most generous of him, indeed." Sammy Jones looked at us, and then said, "I suppose most of you are wondering why Vernon Johnson would do such a thing as this. Well you see, Sampson Cleveland Jones was my father. He served on Mr. Johnson's air crew during World War II."

"Sammy's father was responsible for Vernon surviving the war." Ryan looked directly at Bob and LaVonda. "Isn't that correct, Mr. Jones?"

"Yes, it is. When their aircraft went down in the South Pacific, my father saved Vernon's life, and the two of them then rescued the remaining survivors. If it wasn't for my father's actions, no one would have survived. But after the fact, their commander told them that Vernon would receive sole credit for the heroics, and if either of them tried to tell what really happened, they would both be thrown in the brig. Apparently, the commander's racist streak would not allow for an African-American to be honored."

"And the true story has never been known by anyone?" I asked.

"Only by my immediate family, a few others, and to some degree by Mr. Blakely, here. But your father was quite a man, Mr. Johnson. You should be very proud of what he did. After the war in the 1950s, when very few Negroes, as we were referred to then, were admitted, Vernon came to Topeka and stood up for my father as a character reference and provided information that resulted in his being accepted into the law program there at Washburn University. He is the reason my father became the successful lawyer he was his entire life, and was able to defend the rights of so many disadvantaged people, right up until his own death three years ago. Your father has affected and changed the lives of many by that simple but courageous act, an act that many would have cowered from in those days, and he took no credit for any of it."

Again, we each shook our head at the amazing things we found out about a man we all thought we knew so well.

"Finally," said Ryan, "To you, Bob and LaVonda, Vernon left his hound, Tick, in your care, as well as the farm, all land, personal property, chattel and property attachments."

Bob, LaVonda and I all sighed in relief that there were no surprises here. Maybe Alice had been wrong.

"Except..." continued Ryan.

All of our heads snapped toward Ryan Blakely.

"Except for the mineral rights, which he has bequeathed to Betty Chalmers."

All of our heads snapped to Betty. She looked down at the floor.

"What mineral rights?" asked Bob. "We ain't got no oil wells or nothing like that on the land."

"All I can tell you is what Vernon himself wrote in the will, which is 'Betty will know what to do with whatever proceeds might derive from this venture.'"

"What venture?" Bob was truly upset and LaVonda seemed near tears.

"Betty," I said. "You knew about the guitar. Did you know about this, too?"

She didn't say anything, but continued looking at the floor and avoiding our eyes.

"Betty, is this what you meant when you said 'motive' when we talked the other day? Because if you did, you were right. This really does give you a motive."

She rose slowly and without looking at any of us walked out the office door.

25

There were several roads, all dirt, and no way of telling how many Vernon included or left off his penciled map. I finally came to one that looked like it had been graded by a maintainer recently. At least, no fresh tire marks were on it. The county grader must have also made it to the next one because it was clean too, except for one set of tread showing in the dirt. I turned east and followed the road. It was lined with thick trees and I couldn't see beyond the hedgerow into the fields, but the tire marks made an abrupt turn at a narrow opening and crossed over a rutted area. All that was there was a tumbled-down old farm house. No vehicles. A second line of trees, mostly Junipers and scrub Cedar, stood farther back in and I could see nothing past them.

This looked like as good a possibility as any, and it matched the general description Bonelli had given me as well. I drove down the county road a ways and parked my truck. Then I parted rusty strands of barbed wire, climbed through and started traipsing across the field. But it was slow going. The ground was lousy with jimson weed and tangles of dead undergrowth. By the time I reached the Junipers I was out of breath, so I stopped and peered through.

I couldn't believe the compound of houses and outbuildings that lay hidden behind all the vegetation. And there, next to one of two brick houses, was Thrash's Electra.

I got closer by going from tree to tree and hiding behind a Cedar here and a Juniper there. When I got to the barn I eased my way along one side and rounded the corner in the back. That's when it hit me.

A sour smell, so strong it drove me back, assaulted my nostrils, and I recognized it as that same sewer gas odor from the caked mud on Vernon Johnson's Mercury. I covered my nose with my shirt sleeve, which did nothing to reduce the overpowering smell, and looked around the corner of the barn again. It looked to be an old pig sty fallen into disuse, just like Bob had remembered from the smell. Whoever lived on this place didn't have much use for the property as a working farm, that was for sure. I knew the Little Arkansas had to be nearby, and from where I stood I could see the tree-line of the river across a field, and in-between, a long raised area in the middle of the field. I felt the bones, or an answer to them had to be near, and with them, an answer to Vernon's death.

Car engine noise interrupted my thoughts. I squeezed through a loose board and into the dark barn interior, and at the far end against the blaze of sunlight through the open door a black Denali drove by. The same one from the parking lot at Zingers. By the time I got near the door my eyes adjusted enough that I could see old farm implements, rusted and broken, scattered everywhere. In the corner were objects I readily recognized. I'd seen them often enough. Plastic two liter bottles, tubing, PVC connections, and empty distilled water bottles and tins of acetone. All the paraphernalia needed to cook meth. That was their business, just as Doc Smally had said. Except these objects were all piled in a jumble. Trashed. They, like everything else about this place, looked fallow.

As the door on the Denali slammed, I turned to go back deeper in the shadows of the barn, and when I went around a post which supported a loft area above, there they were. The bones. Heaped up and partially leaning against the post, the empty sockets in its skull stared back at me.

"Hello. Nice of you to pay us a visit, Mr. O'Reilly."

I turned, and there she stood. Clare. She stared at me with the pale pretty side of her face showing and her long black hair covering the purple birth mark. She wore a long black dress, a red and black cowgirl shirt and tooled boots.

"Hello, yourself" I said. "You have an advantage. I don't believe I know you." Except of course, I really did.

"O'Reilly." she said, ignoring my implied question. "That's Irish, isn't it?"

"Yes, it is."

"Me too."

"You still have the advantage."

"Clare. Like the county. You know, County Clare in Ireland. My name is Clare McCabe Miller."

"McCabe. You have a sister," I said.

"Had, yes. Lael. My older sister, Lael. The fair, blond one with the pure voice."

"Whatever happened to Lael McCabe?"

"She went away."

I looked at the bones and asked, "But she returned recently? Unexpectedly?"

"Who would have thought, after all these years?"

I started to put my hand in the pocket that held my holstered Ruger.

"Don't," she said. "I am in possession of two items. One, the keys to your truck, which you so kindly left in the ignition. I came the back way today and ran across it up the road a ways. And two, a small caliber, yet effective, firearm." She raised her dress above the tops of her boots and lifted a handgun out of one of them. If you would be so kind as to relieve yourself of whatever defense you might be carrying." She leveled the handgun at me.

I slowly pulled the Ruger out and tossed it across to her. "Tony Bonelli tells me you murdered Lael."

"So, Mr. Bonelli is talking. Well, that's another situation I will have to remedy. He is correct. I pushed her into the river and watched her drown. Lael. Pure of voice, pure of heart, but with no swimming skills at all. I watched her drift away, downstream and dead, graceful as a floating swan, but a dead floating swan."

"And Vernon Johnson. Did you murder him, too?"

"What a shame, Mr. O'Reilly. He seemed like such a sweet old man, and so earnest in his desire to be helpful. He really thought he was helping us with information about my long lost sister. But he was a fool, a complete fool who understood nothing."

"So what was it? Did he discover all the meth equipment? Was he going to blow the whistle on your operations here?"

She ignored my question. "Now, if you would care to join me in the house," and she motioned with her handgun to precede her.

As we crossed the compound, I said, "I've seen you before. You're the woman who dances with one shoe, like at the Knights of Columbus Hall. Why do you do that? Why do you kick off one of your shoes and dance like that?"

"I don't know. I guess, it's just that everything I do is for shit. I've always felt like I was hobbled anyway, so I just keep turning in the wind, round and round, like an old hobbled mare. Maybe someday I'll get to have both shoes on."

"You have a beautiful voice, Clare. You're beautiful, too. Why would you kill your sister?"

She didn't bother to answer.

When we entered the second brick house, it was like walking into a tomb. All shades and curtains were drawn and a dark gloom prevailed. A window air conditioner hummed continuously pumping stale air into the vault, and it had nowhere to go. I coughed the stagnant air and felt a chill over my body.

Thrash sat on an overstuffed couch drinking a can of beer and he looked up as we walked in. "Who's that?"

She motioned for me to sit in a chair opposite Thrash, and said, "Sweetheart, you haven't been too observant, considering the nature of our enterprise. Mr. O'Reilly here was snooping around the premises."

"O'Reilly? This the dude you been following?"

"The very same," she said and looked at me. "The fishing pond. At Mr. Johnson's farm. Thank you for leading me to my sister's remains. I never would have found that spring house."

I would have shivered at the thought of her stalking me, but I was already frigid in the recycled air conditioning. She laid my Ruger on a table but kept her gun in-hand. Next to the couch where Thrash sat, there was an open cabinet of guns. Scoped rifles as well as 12 and 20 gauge shotguns. None of them had locks. I wondered if they were loaded and ready. I made a mental note for future reference and possible use.

The front door opened and a tall, dark-haired man entered, handsome and with penetrating eyes. He looked at me and then Thrash, but it was Thrash he referred to. "What's he doing here?"

"Business," was all Clare said.

"I don't like it. It's one thing you got a lover and I know it, but you don't have to bring him home and parade him around in front of me."

This was getting interesting. I never realized criminals could have their own personal soap operas.

"Well, Larry, it was just plain unavoidable. Mr. O'Reilly, allow me to introduce you. This is Larry Miller, my good-looking, but really stupid husband."

I didn't offer to shake his hand.

"Stop saying that," Larry said. "I don't like it."

She smiled at him.

"And I'm not stupid."

"You're sweet. But you don't have the brains God gave a piss-ant."

The woman was brutal. Larry glared and then hung his head.

"He is, however, quite strong," said Clare. "Keep that in mind in case you decide to try anything." She housed her gun back inside her boot.

Someone knocked on the peeling varnish of the front door. Clare opened it and I rejoiced. I saw my savior outlined in the fading sunlight in the door. A uniformed police officer stood on the porch. I had no idea how he got there, but I was sure my salvation was at hand. My heart sank when the storm door opened and the glare went off the glass. Phil Turffe walked in and looked around at the group. Wrap-around sunglasses hid his eyes, but he snapped them off like an FBI agent at attention.

"Clare, what's going on here?" he asked, shades dangling from fingertips, and belly hanging over his belt.

"It's a little hard to explain, Phil. Let's see, my husband's upset with me because I brought my lover home, even though it's purely business, and then there's your good friend here, Mr. O'Reilly, who thought he'd drop in for a friendly social call. That about sums it up, Phil. Except, as you know, we are scheduled for one of two Mexican drops sometime in the next hour or so. We got incoming."

"Unh-huh." He twirled his sunglasses around his forefinger, and looked at me. "I told you to stay out of this, but you wouldn't listen, would you?" Then he turned back to Clare. "So, how do we handle this? It's your call, Clare."

"I'm thinking we just grab the money, pack everybody up and head out to the strip."

"Fine," said Phil. "But my point is, what do we do with the private dick?"

"Skip tracer," I corrected him. They ignored me. A beeping sound went off and a red light blinked on one of two small, handheld transceivers sitting on the kitchen counter.

"Okay, that's them," said Clare. "They're in approach. Saddle up, we're riding."

"I don't want him out there with us for the exchange. We need to deal with him now," said Phil.

I looked around. There was Charlie Chan, Dumbo, Deputy Dawg and The Wicked Witch of the West all in one room staring at me, trying to decide my fate. I felt I was in a Looney Tunes rerun. The culmination of Mankind's evolutionary process, the very antithesis of Intelligent Design, culminating at one moment in time in one room in a house, in Kansas, no-less.

I shoved my hand in my pocket and grabbed a fistful of courage as I wrapped my palm around the bloodstone turtle.

"Yeah, what do we do with him?" Larry addressed the group as if he had some authority.

"There's no time. Bring him along for the ride and figure it out later." Clare looked around and motioned to me. "O'Reilly, stand over there."

I moved into the kitchen against an island by the cupboards.

"I want everybody else in the Denali. I'll get the money and we leave in two minutes. Move now."

No one questioned. They moved. They exited and headed for the vehicle. Clare crossed in front of me in the tight space of a cramped kitchen and started to reach up toward the cupboard, for what I guessed was the money for a drug payoff.

When she reached up, she thrust her rear end out and sunk her butt into my groin, pinning me against the island. She paused, wiggled a few times and said, "Oh, Mr. O'Reilly, you surprise me."

"Surprise?" I gasped, her butt still clamped against me.

"Yes, really. You are as hard as a rock."

"Oh," I swallowed hard. "That's my turtle. It's my red speckled turtle."

"I've heard it referred to as a lot of things, but a red turtle? That's a new one."

I started to sweat and hoped someone would walk back in through the door looking for us, but nobody did. I tried reaching for the gun in her boot, but I was pinned solid. She looked over her shoulder at me with her pale pretty side, and then ground her posterior even harder.

"Does your turtle snap? Does it have a long neck?" Then she laughed, pulled a bundle of what I suspected was the drug money from the cupboard, and released me from her rear-end hold.

"Get your ass out the door. We're going to work." She herded me through the door, across the porch and into the Denali.

26

We drove out into the middle of a field of dry grass and jimson weed to the raised area I'd seen earlier. It was an airstrip that looked like a puckered scar on the landscape. The heat of the day still lay on us and a red fireball of a setting sun from the west was on our backs, giving an eerie light to the field as we drove through it.

Everyone got out and stood in a line at one end of the unlit landing area. If anything planned on setting down here, it better be soon. Light was fading and shadows appeared here and there, even in the middle of the open field. Then we heard a far off drone.

A speck in the sky approached low from the south, the drone getting louder and the speck getting bigger. A single-engine came in lower and lower, making its final approach, dipped one wing, righted itself, and started a descent toward us. Five minutes later it stopped at the far end of the strip, turned around and taxied back a bit before coming to a stop.

Clare, who'd been standing next to Thrash, left him, pulled the payment bundle from the car and ran out to the plane as its pilot cut the engine to idle, and Phil stepped back to keep an eye on all of us and the entire situation. I tried to evaluate what was happening too, seeing if any opportunity offered itself up for possible escape. Nothing so far.

The plane's passenger, Hispanic looking, climbed down with a duffel bag, and then unloaded several packages with Clare inspecting them. "Phil," she said. "Take a look at these. She leaned into and across the passenger seat and handed the bundle of money to the pilot as Phil walked over.

I wasted no time. I ran over the far end of the raised strip and across tangles of jimson weed toward the tree-line I assumed to be the Little Arkansas River. It was my one hope. I slid over a precipice and down, down toward the muddy river's edge, where I hoped to float away from my captors and leave them behind on the basin plateau.

Unfortunately, before I hit the water, my body tangled up with the massive roots of a cottonwood that had been blown over in a storm, lay on its side, and sent up shoots in jumbles and knots. I flailed and tried to right myself, but down there in the shadows under a cut-bank, I looked up and saw a flashlight beam above me. Then I heard the voice. It was Phil. How in the hell that fat bastard got there that quickly, I don't know. He heaved and gasped, sucking air in and expelling it from his windpipe.

"Boy, get your ass back up here 'fore I shoot you. Got my flashlight in one hand and my .38 in the other, so don't you try nothing."

Ever since I was a little boy, I did exactly what I was told. Mostly. So I dragged my ass back up that incline and stood looking at Phil and his flashlight and his .38.

"Can you swim, Mr. O'Reilly?" Clare's voice came out of the dark from behind Phil.

"Swim? Yes, yes I can swim." I'd made it back up the incline.

"That's too bad. My sister couldn't. You're standing very close to where Lael went in the water, you know, when I pushed her and she drowned."

"Want me to do him now?" Phil still had the .38 pointed at me.

"Hold your horses, Phil, and put that thing away."

Bless you, Clare. You've redeemed my faith in humanity.

"I told you he was going to be the fly in the ointment. He's going to mess everything up," said Phil.

"You can have him after both drops are complete and then you're in charge of disposing of the remains."

So much for my faith in humanity.

As the plane took off back down the runway, we drove back to the house with one additional passenger. The Hispanic man rode shotgun, and he appeared every bit the stereotypical South-of-the-Boarder Generalissimo, straight out of Central Casting. Battlefield fatigues from head to toe, including the squared cap with bill. Graying, thick mustache and dark stubble on his face. Black holster and handgun strapped to waist.

"Guillermo, as you can see, we have an addition to our group," Clare said, referring to me. "An unwanted addition that we will have to decide what to do with."

Guillermo looked over the seat at me without saying anything. His eyes did not look particularly forgiving.

"Don't be too hasty in your decision," I said. "Remember, even if you get rid of me, you still have another new problem. Bonelli." I said it to see what effect it might have on Guillermo.

He looked at Clare for an explanation, but all she said was, "Later."

Back in the air conditioned mausoleum, Clare sent Larry off to fetch my truck, while Guillermo, who everyone else called by his last name, Roderiguez, let his displeasure be known once he found out the details of me and Bonelli.

"Señora Miller, this is not a good situation. These are not the kinds of, how do you say, complications we expected when we enlisted you to participate in our organization. And do not forget, there is the matter of the second arrival, due early in the morning. This aircraft will be arriving from one of our southern states with the other portion of the merchandise."

While they argued, I casually edged my way to the kitchen table, but my Ruger was no longer there. The least I could do was cop one of the transceivers, so I slipped the one that hadn't gone off in my pocket.

"Let's go. Come with me." Larry had returned and he muscled me off down a hallway, produced some hardware and handcuffed me, one arm to the headboard of a bed.

"You know, Larry," I said, "If it bothers you being a cuckold, I could help you get revenge against Thrash."

"What's a cuckold?" he said.

My God, she was right. He really was stupid. "Never mind," I said.

He looked at me like he wasn't sure what to do next, so he shrugged and walked out.

Light spilled in from the hallway, and on the stand next to me I saw a framed picture, several years old, of three individuals taken at one of the halls on a music night, maybe the Grange. A young Larry stood in the middle with Clare on one side and a blond, presumably Leal, on the other. Their arms wrapped around each other and they all smiled, but Lael's eyes had an innocence about them, while Clare's had a dissembling look in them.

Through the open door, I could hear TV noise and their voices, probably discussing my fate, when and how it would go down. I wondered how long it would take them to discover the missing transceiver. Clare and Roderiguez had both talked about a second drop in the morning, and I wondered if morning meant right after midnight, or sometime later. It must be later, because without a lighted landing strip it would have to be in daylight.

That meant I had several hours to create a reversal of fortune. Or not. And then I would be in the hands of Phil and his .38.

27

I banged my cuff against the headboard and created a racket loud enough to bring Larry back to the room. Divide and conquer strategy, or maybe it was take out the weakest link, I don't know. Anyway, I beckoned, he came. He stood in the doorway.

"What?"

Ah, he was ever so much the glib and loquacious host. "My arm's killing me," I said. "Could you switch the cuffs to the other arm for awhile?"

"Phil's got the key."

"Well, maybe you could like ask to borrow it? Maybe like offer to leave a deposit for security's sake, you know?" I tried to keep it simple. No doubt about it, he was shaping up to prove the weakest link theory. He grunted and left.

Well, the old "arm's killing me trick" didn't work. I pondered my options and hoped I didn't have to swallow sawdust. When Huck Finn and Tom Sawyer tried to free the runaway slave Jim who was chained to a bed, Tom told

Huck they would have to fashion a saw blade, cut off the bed's leg, take the chain off, reposition the leg and put dirt and grease around it to hide the cut. Then Jim would have to eat the sawdust so as not to leave any evidence. Huck pointed out that it would be simpler to just lift the bed's leg and slide the chain off.

I was opting for the simplicity of Huck's approach when Clare appeared and complicated things. Maybe I would have to eat sawdust.

"I understand you are not satisfied with the accommodations," she said.

"I'm used to the deluxe suite at the Hilton."

"My, my. Why don't you let me entertain you?" She picked up a guitar that leaned against a dresser, sat on a tall stool in the corner and began strumming softly. "It'll help pass the time until…" She shrugged.

"You never answered my question? Why did you kill your sister?" I asked.

She continued playing while she talked. "She was older than me by a year, and had the pure voice, and was blond and prettier with no marks on her face and Larry fancied her more than me. And I had to have him. Larry, the Miller's boy, tall and handsome. And quiet. I mistook the quiet and those deep penetrating eyes of his for a piercing knowledge of the soul. I was young and ignorant and didn't understand until later that it wasn't a piercing knowledge, it was pure stupidity. That boy is as empty as a barn in August. Everybody here knows what happened to my sister except him. He still thinks Lael just ran off to find fame. I guess I got what I deserved."

She started singing an old folk song along with the refrain she'd been playing. It was a song of death. Mine, I supposed.

Oh death oh death, please give me time,
To fix my heart and change my mind.

Your mind is fixed, your heart is bound,
I've got the shackles to drag you down.

She stopped playing. "I'm disappointed it's come to this, Mr. O'Reilly. The whole time I've watched you, from the Johnson's place to the fishing pond and all, even though we've been adversaries, I've grown a sort of affection for you."

I felt a chill run up my spine at the thought of being stalked by her and watched these last several days.

"I often thought as I watched you, that you and me, well, you know." She brushed her hand across her forehead, as if she was brushing away her thoughts like she would a cobweb. Then she sang another verse.

I've come for to get your soul,
Take your body and leave it cold.
I'll drop the flesh from off'n your frame,
The earth and the worms both have their claim.

She put the guitar down, walked to the side of the bed and leaned over letting her long black hair fall across my face, and the white cheek brush across my lips. "I bet you'd make a good ride, Mr. O'Reilly. I surely do bet you would."

My God. Her husband and lover were both in the other room, and now this. The woman was relentless.

She stood, abruptly, and her voice took on a hard edge. "It's probably for the best," she said. "It would have only complicated matters. I don't even know what I'm going to do with Larry, now that he's become so useless. You men are such a burden. And, considering what must happen in the morning, it doesn't much matter, does it?" She walked to the door.

"This is kind of embarrassing," I said. "But, I gotta pee. Real bad."

She stared for a second and then turned to leave.

"If you want a wet mattress that's your business."

She walked out without saying another word. Such compassion. But a few seconds later, Larry came in with a key, undid the cuffs and escorted me down the hall to a bathroom. He walked in with me.

"Could I have a little privacy?"

"Okay, but I'm leaving the door open a crack," he said. "I hear a window open, I'll be in here in a flash and I'll hurt you."

"Ouch." I waited until he'd closed the door, except for the crack. After I flushed, I turned on the water and made as if I was washing my hands, but I went through the drawers and under the sink."

"Let's go," he said.

"I'm just washing up. Keep your pants on." I finally found what I was looking for. A bobby pin. I straightened it and put it in the opposite pocket from the arm that had been manacled and walked out.

Back in the bedroom I held my arm out but he took the other one.

"Thought you wanted to switch arms. You said it was killing you."

"Oh, yeah." Damn. He cuffed the opposite arm this time and walked out.

Now, with the bobby pin in the same pocket as my cuffed arm, I had to reach across my body with the free hand, twist it down and into the pocket and fish around. I had to put torque into the cuffed arm, which hurt, and I couldn't get enough purchase with my fishing fingers to pull the pin out of my pocket. It took several minutes of squirming and wriggling, but I finally got it.

The cuffs looked to be an older pair of Smith and Wesson's, so they probably weren't double locks, which is good, because it would have made it harder. If I had a shim, I could have fiddled around and released the pawl on the lock fairly quickly. But all I had was the bobby pin, which meant I had to poke around and try to release each cog on the ratchet, cog-by-cog.

I'd gotten three releases and the cuff was getting larger, but not enough to slip out of yet, when I heard footsteps in the hall. I laid out straight and palmed the pin. Larry looked in, checking on me, didn't say anything, and left. It took me about another ten minutes of work to get the cuff where I finally slipped my hand through it, rubbed some feeling back into my wrist and hopped out of the bed, free and clear.

The bedroom window was a double hung, and it opened easily. No screen, and I was out and on the ground with virtually no noise. I slipped around to the front of the house where they had brought my truck, reached up under the frame where I keep a magnetized box with an extra key, and then retrieved an ice pick that I always keep in the cab. Using the ice pick, I popped one tire on each of their vehicles, hoping the whoosh of air couldn't be heard inside the house over the constant buzz of the air conditioning unit.

I'd just done the last tire, the Denali, when I heard Larry's voice yell from inside the house. He must have been doing one of his periodic checks on me.

"He's gone, God dammit. The window's open and he's gone. God dammit."

I ran to my truck and cranked the engine, just as someone came out the front door. It was Phil and he had a shotgun in-hand. I gunned it and spun out, fishtailing past the house, leaning away and ducking to one side. That's when I heard the report. It was deafening. My passenger-side and rear windows shattered and covered me in a hail of glass, and I felt a stinging sensation in my shoulder.

I was a good fifty yards past him, so I hoped the scattergun had indeed scattered, but I felt a weakening in my shoulder. My truck veered driver's-side and skidded into the edge of the barn. Phil must have had a single-shot instead of a side-by-side, or an over-under, because I could see him in my rearview, fumbling and trying to reload. The others poured out of the house around him.

I jammed the stick in reverse, threw it into first and popped the clutch, throwing up a rooster tail of dust as I spun out and away from the yard. Phil, having reloaded, fired again, but I was far enough away that the scatter pattern didn't catch any part of me or the truck. As I turned on the county road I could hear their shouts of profanity in the background when they discovered the deflated tires on each vehicle.

I got woozy as I drove toward Chisholm and I felt the truck angling across the centerline. I looked over my shoulder. Blood spread across the cloth on the back of my bench seat, but there wasn't a lot of it. Some of the pellets must have got me, but I didn't know what gauge the shotgun was or how many pellets hit me or how deep they went.

I made the edge of Chisholm and then I remember seeing the Mobley Mobile station sign. I think I recall seeing Allen Mobley. Then it all went black.

28

"You say there were human bones in a barn?"

"Yes, Sir, I did."

"And you say there was some South American general present?" The officer had quit taking notes and just stared at me while I nodded in the affirmative.

They had taken me to St. Joe's in Wichita, and when I woke I had been on a table in the emergency room. I'd had three 00 buck load pellets removed from my shoulder and had been told I was lucky, they were mostly superficial wounds. The fact that I had been a moving target, that there had been glass as an intermediate obstruction and that the distance between the shooter and target was substantial, all contributed to lessening the severity of my wounds.

Now I lay in a room talking to a uniformed officer because they insisted on keeping me for observation, at least overnight, even though I objected strenuously. The officer who was interviewing me scratched his chin.

Still dazed and disconnected from present reality to some degree, I couldn't tell if my tumbled hodgepodge of details about the Miller place and where I thought it was and the lady with a birth mark and the drugs and bones and Phil-the-policeman, made any sense at all. The expression on the officer's face told me it didn't. He looked at me as if I was some alien who just stepped off a space ship, or maybe he thought I was human, but I was the crazy guy building the big mound of mashed potato stuff in "Close Encounters of the Third Kind."

He looked at my bloodstone turtle sitting on the stand next to my bed, head outstretched and staring back at him, like I was a child in need of consoling. I shifted in bed and adjusted my hospital gown so I couldn't feel my bare butt on the sheets. It made me feel more like a grownup.

"You say you're a friend of Lieutenant Daniels?" he said, while keeping his gaze on my turtle instead of me.

"Unh-huh."

"I'll let her know."

I don't know if they gave me something to make me sleep or if I just crashed on my own, and I don't know how much later it was when I woke up, but Charlie was standing at the foot of my bed, hands on her hips, staring down at me.

"Hey, Bruiser," she said, as I woke and blinked my eyes. "I brought you a present." She held up a forest green tee-shirt with WPD stenciled across the front. "I heard you might be in need of a new shirt. Something about an old shirt of yours having some holes in it."

"Thanks, Charlie."

"I also hear you been telling tall tales to one of Wichita's finest."

"Yeah." I was still a little groggy.

"You know, when you decide to go after all the bad guys in the world, and to do it all by your own little self, it causes a whole shit-load of problems for a whole lot of the rest of us."

"I don't know what it is Charlie, I just seem to draw the scum of the earth."

"So that's why I'm attracted to you? I'm not sure I like that theory. Listen, there's a bunch of people that have been concerned about you, and you went off and left them in the lurch. I talked with Laura this morning. She's worried sick. You might give us mere mortals a little consideration part of the time."

"Sorry," I said, looking out my window at a brick wall. I couldn't look her in the eye.

"The report details turned in by the officer who interviewed you, and I use the term 'interview' loosely, are somewhat vague." She sat down in the chair next to my bed. "I thought maybe my stunning beauty and charismatic presence might make you a bit more coherent. Tell me what happened."

After I finished what was definitely a more lucid account, and given her a fairly good idea of the Miller compound location, by the time she left, she made several calls that effected action from multiple state and local forces across Kansas. The Miller place was probably vacated by now, but it would soon be crawling with uniforms.

As she stood in the door to go, she said, "I talked with that Mobley kid who called EMS for you. You know, he rode in with you in the wagon. Stayed with you until he knew you'd be okay."

A vague recollection of seeing Allen Mobley came back to me. "He wasn't here when I regained consciousness in ER."

"Well, he's got your truck. Said he'd have it fixed for you when they boot you out of here. Oh, and give Laura a call. If she's not at her place, she'll be at Janie's. She's been taking good care of the kid. By the way, when am I slated for some action?"

"Tomorrow night. My place. Seven o'clock sharp." I don't know where it came from, I just blurted it out. I grabbed the bloodstone turtle and put it on my chest.

She'd already started out the door, but stopped dead in her tracks and turned back, her brown eyes big. "Lorna Doone. My ship's come in. You're not pulling my leg now, are you O'Reilly?" She looked at me with a big smile, shook her head and as she walked off, said, "Oh I'll be there. With bells on. Seven sharp. Cats couldn't drag me away."

Before I tried calling Laura, I went into the bathroom. When I came out an orderly in green scrubs was at the closet with his back to me.

"Hey, Buddy, you don't know when they might kick me loose from here, do you?" I said.

He turned around slowly and had my pants in his hands. It was then I noticed my room door had been closed and the chair shoved under the doorknob.

"You're not really an orderly are you?" He just stared at me. "Did you stay at a Holiday Inn last night?" No response, just the stare. "What are you doing?"

"You got something of ours," he said. He had a raspy voice, was dark and shorter than me but stocky, with a scar under one eye. He looked like a Samoan Mosquito Dancer I had known in college who could slap the shit out of you with one hand. He dropped my pants on the floor and pulled a leather blackjack out from under his baggy scrubs. "Mr. Roderiguez wants his transceiver back."

I'd been right. Roderiguez's eyes were not forgiving.

"You must have me mistaken for somebody else." I flashed my Irish grin, but it didn't take. Even as I said it, my eyes went involuntarily to the stand with my turtle on it where the rest of my effects, along with what he wanted, had been stored in the drawer.

His Polynesian eyes shifted there, too, and I claimed the advantage. In that split second of eye movement, I was on him and took him down, but even though he was smaller than me, he was able to partially raise his hand with the blackjack and bring it down on my lower back. It was only a quarter-swing but it took the breath out of me and stung like hell, shooting pain up into my shoulder wounds.

I gasped for air and at the same time managed to pin his weapon arm down, twisting his wrist back hard and around, until I heard it snap. He yelled in pain and I grabbed the blackjack from him. While he rolled around on the floor, I pulled the tie and dropped my hospital gown, had my clothes on and gotten all my stuff out of the drawer. Forty-five seconds max.

"You like my new shirt? It was a present from a friend." He was still moaning in pain. "This what you looking for?" I held the transceiver up. It was blinking red. I pocketed it and said, "Tell Roderiguez he can have it and the blackjack when I get my Ruger back. You might tell him it's blinking, too."

He was on his knees now, trying to right himself with his good hand, but when he reached under his scrubs again, I didn't wait to see what he might produce. I whipped the blackjack, full force, across his shoulder and sent him sprawling and back against the wall.

"Don't worry," I said as I walked out the door. "They take real good care of you here. You got Blue Cross?"

I checked myself out of St. Joe's and called a cab. I made the rounds of my usual haunts, rounding up the usual suspects: cheeses, breads, specialty items for sauces for Saturday night's intended rendezvous with Charlie. The cabbie balked at driving me all the way up to Chisholm, but when I told him there was a big tip in for him he took off and didn't say a word the rest of the way. He dropped me off at the Mobley station.

Allen was stocking cans of Pennzoil on a shelf in one of the bays when he saw me get out of the cab.

"Are you okay?" His eyes got wide like he couldn't believe I was up and about.

"Yeah. I'm a tough old bird, Allen."

"I've never seen anything like that. Your truck rolled up and hit the curb and you were slumped over and I saw the blood. I was really scared."

"Thanks for what you did, Allen. They told me you rode in with me and EMS. I really appreciate that. Speaking of my truck, do you know when it might be ready?"

"Oh, it's drivable now. The glass is all replaced, but you'll have to take it to a body shop for the dent in the front end. And I couldn't get all the blood out of the seat."

That Allen. An amazing kid.

When I got home, I shelved the groceries and then called Bomber Jackson, apologized for being incommunicado, and picked up a trace job he had waiting for me. I really did intend to walk the straight-and-narrow and get back to business as usual, especially after Charlie's tirade that made me feel about two-years old.

Then again, if Roderiguez and crew needed the transceiver badly enough to send a goon after me, something was amiss. It blinked a constant red. Maybe the second plane went down and its transponder was sending out its location. They'd be desperate for the little device if that was the case.

I called Laura and updated her. I had misgivings about my Charlie date, so I asked Laura and Janie to join us all on Saturday night for a celebration of my return. She informed me that Francine had materialized, minus Jerry Clawson, and ought to be present, too.

Exhausted and sore, my lower back still partially numb from the blackjack slap and my shoulder with a constant sting, I fixed some simple bruschetta and kicked back with a glass of red.

I couldn't get Roderiguez's goon out of my mind, and the transceiver still blinked its intermittent red on my reading table. Somewhere out there, a transponder waited to be found.

Roderiguez, or maybe Clare, would come. It was just a matter of time.

29

"**God dammit, Jimmy, where the hell you been?**" Sheriff Jake Alexander's voice boomed from the opening of Clare Miller's barn.

I'd been called out to help with some of the questions KBI had while combing the place and carting off the drug paraphernalia.

"Question is, where the hell you been, Alex?"

"I would've been back soon as I heard what was going on, but that damned tropical storm or hurricane or whatever the hell it was moved through Florida. Mavis and me, we couldn't get a flight out for the life of us. Spent the night at the airport eating Twinkies out of machines and sucking down canned beer at the bar."

Jake Alexander is a little older than me and he's a large man, maybe six-four. He's big. Not fat like Phil, because he carries it well. He doesn't have a lot of muscle, but he has weight and he knows how to throw it. Legend has it that he's never lost an arm wrestling contest in his fifty-some years of existence, and I believe it. He's got a droopy mustache that always looks like it needs trimming and it usually has bits of food debris hanging in it, and his eyebrows are large, dark and bushy. Nothing about the man is small, not even his voice.

"Well, it's good to have you back," I said, shuddering at the thought of canned beer.

"Good to be back. I heard what happened to you. You alright?"

I nodded. "Raring to go," I said.

"Sorry I wasn't here to deal with all of this. What the hell happened anyways?"

I tried, best I could to bring him up to speed on what he hadn't learned already, while KBI officers unloaded equipment and protective suits to deal with the meth lab junk.

"I been reading the reports, Jimmy, but I just don't understand it all, and I know it's still ongoing. But first this business of Phil being dirty. And then there's this Vernon Johnson thing. I just can't get a handle on it. I knowed there was bad boys around here, but what's it all coming to?"

"I don't know myself, Alex." I tried to reassure him, but then, I really didn't know.

"Yeah." He stared off for a few seconds. "You're not trying to do anything foolish-like, are you?" Alex looked me in the eye. "Like trying to take on the world and solve this all by yourself, maybe?"

"I'm just getting by, day-by-day, Alex. Like I always try to do."

"Well, we'll keep an eye out. But what with the situation with Phil and all, we're down a man. It's just me and Jack now, but we'll do the best we can. We're going to get these people, Jimmy."

A woman in a blue KBI tee-shirt called for me to come over to the house. When I left him, Alex looked shaken, just nodding his head.

By the time Charlie arrived for dinner at seven sharp Saturday evening, everyone else I'd invited had already showed up, too. If Charlie was disappointed that Laura, Janie and Francine had been invited, she didn't show it. I did feel sheepish at the deception though, but she was a good sport about it.

By then, I also had updates on the results of Charlie's phone calls from the hospital room. Joint forces of KBI and local law enforcement had, at various times, entered the police station in Chisholm, interviewed Jack Sampson and found out that Officer Phil Turffe had not been seen or heard from since he checked in for duty late Thursday night, and his cruiser was also missing; returned to Clawson's place near Quivera Refuge and found nothing additional beyond the fertilizer bags on their previous raid; and descended on the Miller compound north of Chisholm where I had helped them and they found the bones and old meth paraphernalia.

If my count was correct, there were now two dead, Lael and Vernon, and there were five fugitives, whereabouts unknown: Clare, Larry, Thrash, Phil and Roderiguez. I felt uneasy about the five fugitives and what they might be up to, but it was a good thing I didn't know. If I'd had prior knowledge of the events to come as well as how my resolve to return to the boring straight-and-narrow life would fade fast, I could never have looked Charlie in the eye at dinner that night.

Saturday's dinner began with a toast. I poured a Conundrum white to go with my crostini appetizer of goat cheese, tomatoes, basil and olive oil. And I convinced Janie to forego her penchant for Pepsi and try a bottle of San Pellegrino sparkling water.

"Wow," she said. "This makes my nose tickle. I like it."

We toasted to all of us being together, alive and safe, and to what good fortune there was that we did have in this world. We sat down to a first course of cantaloupe and prosciutto, and then continued with the Conundrum and San Pellegrino. Laura sat at one end of the table, her slim frame dressed in a designer outfit of red and black. Black silk blouse, red blazer, and black slacks with red pumps, her auburn hair twisted in a French braid. Charlie sat at the other end, her sturdy round face highlighted by dark hair, cropped short. She wore a blazer, too, a navy cotton one over a white cotton shirt and khaki slacks. Francine and Janie sat opposite me, with Francine dressed far beyond what I'd ever seen her in before, black denim pants and a white knit pullover. She had heavy makeup that looked like it covered a bruise on her right cheek. Janie was wearing what was probably the only dress she ever owned, a cotton print that Mom most likely purchased from the DAV.

The mood was light and when my CD exchanger shifted from Mario Frangoulis to Rachmaninoff, I have eclectic tastes, I brought in the main course, strozzapreti pasta tossed lightly with a Portobello and porcini sauce, topped with shredded asiago. I went US style and served the field greens with the main course figuring no one would object, and as one might expect, I uncorked a fine red Brunello to go with it. Laura, ever-vigilant, brought some Bud Light, knowing Francine would prefer that.

My French doors to the terrace were open and a cool evening breeze brought whiffs of herbs into the room. We laughed a lot while making light of recent events, but I finally had to ask Charlie what the deal was with the Millers and drugs.

"DTOs," she said.

"What's that?" Janie asked.

"Drug trafficking organizations. They're mostly Mexican, and they're high-dollar, well-structured groups with a lot of muscle. They look for just the right people to bring in their goods to, mostly meth, and the locals, like the Millers, take all the heat for distributing it. The Millers had apparently been cooking their own for a year or two, and decided to go big-time by affiliating with a DTO."

I looked at Charlie. "Maybe I've been out of the loop too long, but how could some mom and pop locals like the Millers distribute that much dope?"

"They usually have multiple peddlers. Like Thrash for the music scene. They probably got at least one OMG lined up."

"What's an OMG?" Janie again.

"Lorna Doone," she said. "Those are outlaw motorcycle gangs. There's several operating in the area, and they can sweep into a town, urban or rural, and deal it off in short order, and on a lower profile than you'd think."

That prompted an entire discussion of what the term Lorna Doone meant, and Charlie had to explain how way back when, in college, in order to get her degree in AJ, she had to take an English class that she absolutely dreaded. But the instructor made them read a Romance novel by the name of Lorna Doone. She not only loved the story of the outlaw Doone family, she was enchanted by the sound of the name itself. Charlie adopted the name as her mantra, her expression of all that truly amazed her. "Lorna Doone," she said again, as she finished off the last sip of her Brunello.

I ended the dinner with a simple desert, scoops of vanilla ice cream with green crème de menthe poured over the top, and an almond biscotti stuck in it. We all went into the living room afterward with some coffee and tea.

Francine apologized to Janie and all of us for her absence, and told Janie, "I promise, I'm going to be a better mother to you than what I been. I never should have taken up with that asshole. Pardon my French. I shouldn't use words like that around you. I promise I'm going to quit smoking, too. And I'll start going to your games. And I'm going to get you that puppy you been wanting."

"Whoa," said Laura. "Take it easy there. That's an awful lot of promising. You'd better go slowly with all that."

"I will, but I really mean it. And I want to thank you and Mr. O'Reilly for looking out for my Janie. I really appreciate that."

Janie smiled at her mother and I saw tears in her eyes. "I'll be here sometime in the morning, Mr. 'O,' to straighten things up."

After everyone left and I lay in bed wondering at the innocence of youth, I thought I heard movement outside my window. I lay still for a long time, and for awhile it seemed like maybe it was just the wind in the trees, but just when I was convinced it was that and only that, it shifted and sounded more like a human or an animal moving around. I got up, went to the French doors clad only in my BVDs, and stepped out onto the terrace. Nothing. Wind. Pure imagination.

When I woke up Sunday morning, I did a section run and then worked the weights and bags. After a cool down, I showered and dressed, and as an after-thought, I went out back and looked around. Under my bedroom window the dirt had been disturbed. No footprints or animal tracks, but someone or something had definitely had a presence there. I don't know how a person knows these kinds of things, but I did. It was a feminine presence.

Instead of fixing breakfast, I walked into town, got a Sunday paper and a coffee-to-go at Latte Dottie's, then went across Commercial to the square. The Catholics were headed north and the Methodists south in their weekly ritual, each toward their respective houses of worship, nodding to one another politely as they passed. It was a sort of small-town mid-America version of an Italian passeggiata, but without their sense of fashion.

Strains of organ music drifted from both directions and mingled, indistinguishable from one another, as each denomination ensconced themselves in their pews. I read the paper and sipped coffee while sitting on my own hardwood park bench of a pew. There was a fresh, cool breeze and heavy dew on the grass. Everything felt clean.

The front door was open when I returned, so Janie had arrived and was hard at work. I announced my presence.

"I'm back, Janie. I'm going in to do some computer work."

I didn't get a response, so I walked out the open French doors onto the terrace. She wasn't there either, but the watering can lay on its side and the faucet was turned on with water running out of my garden hose.

"Janie?" I called out. I searched the house and she was nowhere to be found. Then I saw the book of Yeats poems. It was splayed open and wedged under a table leg. When I picked it up, I saw a page had been torn out. I checked the table of contents. The title of the missing poem was "The Stolen Child," Yeats' poem about a kid who was taken away from the human world by fairies.

My neck muscles tightened and my heart went cold.

30

I banged hard on Francine's door until she answered. She stood in the open door, sleepy-eyed and still in her nightshirt.

"Where's Janie?" I said, through the screen door.

"Prob'ly at your place, Mr. O'Reilly. Said last night she was going over early to get her work done."

I opened the door and brushed past her without asking permission. "Check the house. I'll look out back."

"What's wrong?"

"Jerry Crawford's taken her," I said, after we'd searched her house and yard. "That ex-boyfriend of yours, who is a registered sex offender, has taken Janie." I tried not to be accusatory, but it was in my voice. She stood, helpless, just staring at me.

"Look," I said. "I know he wouldn't go back to his place in Rice County. Where else might he have gone?"

"I don't know, honest, I don't." She had panic in her eyes now.

"Where were you at with him?"

"We was in Colorado. He delivered some stuff out there to some people he called a Posse or a Comitatus or something. He used to meet with some of them here in that old Grange Hall they shut up after they built the new one."

"Listen," I said. "You call Sheriff Alexander and tell him exactly what's happened. If Jack Sampson is on duty, tell him to call Alex. I'm going out there to the old hall now. There's not a minute to waste."

She looked confused, but nodded, and I was out the door and headed west out of town. That's when a tan four-door zoomed past, cut in front of me and stopped dead. I slammed on my breaks as two men got out and faced me.

I instinctively reached for the push-button cutaway under the dash and realized I was no longer in possession of my Ruger, and I'd failed to put one of my other weapons there in its place. In fact, I'd hidden the transceiver there. One of the two men stared through the window at me.

I hopped out facing them and made a mental note of the license number. They were two of the blandest looking individuals I'd ever seen. Two absolutely non-descript men. Nothing about either one distinguished them. Neither one was tall, nor short. Neither was fat or thin, light or dark. Both were underdressed in jeans, tee-shirt and light jacket. One had light sandy hair, the other dark sandy hair.

"You the Bobbsey Twins?" I said. They stared, blank faces, no sense of humor. "Sorry boys. I'm in a hurry." I started to get back in my truck.

"It'll have to wait."

"Emergency," I said.

"We got a bathroom where we're going." This from the light sandy haired one.

I reached in my open door and behind the seat for the baseball bat I keep there. The dark sandy haired one brought a nine out of his jacket, aimed it at me and said,

"Nope. Make this easy on yourself. We don't have a lot of time. We've got real important duties down in Wichita."

"Look guys, this is really important. Maybe a life or death situation." I flexed my jaw.

"So's this. Maybe yours," said Light Sandy. He pushed me into the backseat of the tan four door.

Light Sandy drove and I sat in the back with Dark Sandy.

"What's this all about?" I said, but my mind raced on, thinking about Janie and her possible fate with Jerry Crawford. If Francine got Alex, maybe he could be there in time. My mastoids and capitis tightened.

"Somebody wants to talk with you," said Dark Sandy as he put one of those giant sleeping blindfolds on me.

"Mind telling me who? I don't like being in the dark."

But neither one said anything. They didn't laugh either. In my sightless world, I felt like Tiresias. I lost track of the number of turns we made, what direction we went, and how many times we went from paved to gravel to hardpan and back. I was lost.

"This have anything to do with the Polynesian guy?" I said.

"Sua-Lua?" said Dark Sandy, and he actually snickered a couple of times. "He'd be here himself, but unfortunately, he suffered a job related injury."

Maybe he had a sense of humor after all. "Hey, I'd be glad to apologize to him," I said. But we rode in silence the rest of the way and a band tightened across my forehead with pain encircling my head.

When the blindfold came off, we'd stopped in a large gravel drive and parking lot in front of a house in some rural area. I heard the pops of a gun firing somewhere.

As my eyes throbbed from the corded muscles in my neck, they adjusted to light, and I saw Sua-Lua's squat, thick torso huffing his way to the car. His injured arm was in a wrist cast, and he opened my door with the good arm, then reached in and with one powerful move pulled me up, out and thrust me on the ground.

"No rough stuff," said Light Sandy. "Unless he doesn't cooperate. Boss's orders."

"How's things in Pago Pago?" I said, dusting myself off. "Sorry about the wrist. Nothing personal, you know. It was just business."

Sua-Lua glared at me and then croaked out in that raspy voice of his, "You gonna get yours."

"You gargle with Drano in the mornings?" I said.

He grabbed my arm and muscled me around to the back of the house. The Bobbsey Twins disappeared. Tree lines bordered the place everywhere, some straight, some curved and wandering. The curved ones might be a river or a stream, or maybe not. No distinguishable landmarks or towers. There was no telling where we were.

The gunshots came from a firing range where someone shot at a figure of a human torso on a weighted paper target that had been drawn out on a pulley to the end of the line. As I got closer, I could see the bullet cluster, all the holes neatly impacted in and around the heart.

"Good shooting," I said to Sua-Lua. He propelled me the last few feet to the shooter, who turned and faced me.

"Thank you. I've had a great deal of practice, and I always use excellent quality weapons," said Gulliermo Roderiquez. He held up the handgun for me to see, my Ruger. "The only problem with this is, five shots and you must reload. I find this is not very practical."

"It works for me," I said. "I didn't recognize you in your new togs."

"My what?"

"Your clothes. You ditched the generalissimo costume." He was dressed all in black. Black linen slacks, black soft cotton tee with an incredibly high thread count, and a sports coat that matched the trousers. "What's this all about, Roderiguez?"

"I think you know. It is necessary to return the transceiver to me."

"Sorry, don't know what you're talking about."

"Then you have a poor memory. You showed it to your friend here, Sua-Lua."

"Damn, that short term memory loss. It happens with age. Oh yeah, I forgot, I, ah, turned it over to the authorities."

"I doubt that seriously, Mr. O'Reilly. Let us be practical men. I have something of value that you want, and you have something of value that I want. Surely we can come to an agreement."

"I would like my Ruger back. I'm very sentimental about it, but I don't think it has quite the same street value as the contents of your downed airplane."

He looked at me, puzzled, and then handed me the revolver. "A show of good faith, then, on my part. You do not comprehend, do you? I would not, how do you say? bicker, over such a trivial matter. No, it is not that. You must understand, and understand clearly. We have the young lady, Mr. O'Reilly."

His statement jolted me. I actually had to pause and think for a moment.

"Janie?" My heart caught in my throat. Shit, it wasn't Crawford, and Alex was on a wild goose chase right now. Why hadn't I seen this coming? "You have Janie?" I said. My head felt like a steal band was being tightened around it.

"I thought you understood that," he said. "I am sorry, that is my fault."

"I want to see her."

"She is not available."

Bring her out and let me see that she's okay." I rubbed my temples.

"The girl is not at this location." He said it emphatically.

"I need proof," I said.

"She is being taken care of at what will remain an undisclosed location. I can provide proof after we make the arrangements for our exchange. I can provide another kind of proof to you now, though."

He snapped his fingers at Sua-Lua, who walked to the house and emerged a moment later with the Bobbsey Twins dragging a terrified man out to the firing range.

"In case you doubt what will happen to the girl, I show you that I will not hesitate to kill her if our arrangements are not concluded. Age or gender has nothing to do with it. This is Felipe. I brought him here as a trusted helper, but he chose to take some of the proceeds from our street sales. He has been a great disappointment to me."

The two goons had Felipe in front of the paper target and held him rigidly while he tried to twist free, a look of horror on his face. Roderiguez calmly took a nine millimeter out of his coat, quickly steady his aim and fired one shot to the center of Felipe's forehead. My own head snapped back, a reflex action. The two goons didn't even flinch. Felipe slumped to the ground between them and they dragged him away.

"I hope my demonstration convinces you of my earnestness."

"It does," I said, grimly. Then I added, "I also need you to give up Clare Miller."

"That is not a possibility. She is providing a valuable service for us at the moment and has shown complete loyalty."

"I'll be damned if I'm going to let Vernon Johnson's murderer go free."

"That is the deal. You may take it or leave it."

"I don't think you're in that kind of a bargaining position, Roderiguez. You're a lieutenant. You're up here to make sure the operation runs smoothly for the big boys south of the border. If you lose the goods in that plane, I'd say your fate might be similar to Felipe's."

"Do you care to wager the girl's life on that?" When I didn't answer, he said, "From the time they drop you off, you have twenty four hours set up the exchange. Then I kill her."

"How do I get in touch with you?"

"You don't. We will be in touch with you."

"I'm not going to sit by the phone, you know."

"That is your business." He nodded to the boys and Sandy Light and Sandy Dark escorted me back to the tan four door. I wondered if a finger snap meant kill and a nod meant take him away.

When the blindfold came off the second time, I stood next to my truck back in Chisholm, with exactly twenty four hours to resolve Janie's fate. I rubbed my temple and felt the chill of the execution I'd just witnessed settling in my bones.

31

Forty-five minutes later, Laura walked through my front door, dressed to kill. Literally. No coordinated silk outfit this time, but dark, loose-fitting work clothes suitable for throwing kicks, laying low or firing a weapon. She had one accessorizing item of jewelry though.

"You into arts and crafts now?" I nodded to a necklace she wore, the phalanx tuning peg I'd given her, attached to a leather strip around her neck.

"We're both in this for Janie. You're avenging Vernon's murder, and this..." she touched the finger bone, "this is for Lael. She deserves some justice too."

"Better late than never."

"I said it on the phone, but I want to be perfectly clear," she said. "The only reason I'm partnering with you is because of the situation with Janie. And that is also predicated on your acceptance of this."

She tossed a cell phone to me. "I bought it cheap at Wal-Mart. You can junk it when this is over if you want, but we stay in constant communication throughout." She showed me how to make a call with it and also how to text message.

"Here's the plan," I said, sweating while I fingered the cell phone.

"You got a plan? I'm impressed, O'Reilly."

"We'll both be fully armed. You'll track Clare and her crew on the music and drug scene to see if they lead us back to Roderiguez and Janie. If and when the time is appropriate, we take Clare down for Vernon's murder, but Janie's top priority. I'm going to follow my lead and hope it takes me directly to Janie." I explained the license number from the tan four door that I had a friend at DMV trace. "If either one of us deems it necessary, the other one leaves and goes immediately to help with the situation at hand."

"The tan four door? Aren't they just goons for Roderiguez?" she said.

"Exactly. And they said they had what they called duties down in Wichita. Duties they didn't seem particularly happy about. Like maybe guarding an adolescent."

"You call Charlie?"

"No."

"How about Alex?"

"No."

"That bothers me O'Reilly."

"What can I say? Janie's life's on the line. My decision."

I laid out the arsenal I'd unlocked from my cabinet, had taken the locks off of and assembled. I divvied it up, along with the ammunition. We each walked away with one 9 mm Baby Eagle semiautomatic handgun and extra clips with fifteen rounds each, as well as one assault rifle. I added one scoped rife with night vision, as well as two-way radios with headsets. I also provided a dirk for each of us to be housed in a waist sheath. And I was now once again in possession of my beloved Ruger. In addition, Laura brought her Jo, an Aikido staff, and we loaded rappelling and climbing equipment into each of our vehicles, just in case. Hey, you never know. Now, if we only knew where we were going and what we were looking for.

I felt like a corpse. All dressed up and nowhere to go.

I changed the message on my voice mail to let anyone calling know, specifically Roderiguez, that I could now be reached at such-and-such a cell phone number. We each had a cooler with sandwiches and bottled water.

It looked like it might be a long day and night, so I set the alarm, and we each took a two hour nap, me on the couch, her on my bed.

While I napped, I dreamed, and in my dream a blind turtle took me on a journey. Tiresias ferried me across waters to the Underworld where the dead of Odysseus, his mother, Hercules and others waited for me to ask them questions. They were mere shades, ashes of themselves and held no answers. But Sondra, my wife, waited for me there too, and my dreams were filled with hair the color of ripened wheat and the soft scent of pine needles. Sondra's voice came to me from the tender belly of the turtle's Underworld. It was gentle and reassuring, like the fragrance of her hair, and it said that everything would be fine. She told me there was an abiding peace.

"Find it," she whispered. "Find your abiding peace."

When I awoke, rested, Tiresias slept next to the couch, his head withdrawn into his shell. I got up and checked the French doors. They stood ajar, just wide enough for Ty to have entered. I lifted him gently, both hands supporting his underbelly, and carried him out into the safety of his terrace habitat, depositing him amongst the basil. The corded knot in my neck had been released and there was no band around my forehead.

I wondered at the way of the world, and whether an Ornate Box Turtle living today on the plains of Kansas could really have any understanding, any ancestral knowledge, of the scheme of things.

What was it Frost wrote in that poem of his? Was he correct, was there a "Design" that superseded any human concern or concept? "What brought the spider to these heights?" Indeed. What design brought the turtle to me?

After Laura woke, we loaded the coolers with the rest of our equipment.

We each left in our separate prized vehicle. We exchanged cell phone numbers. We vowed to keep in touch. It reminded me of high school graduation. "Don't ever change," I said, as she got into her 'Vette. She shook her head in silence.

I parked outside the address I'd gotten for the tan four door from my friend at DMV. The car was registered to a John Smithson, about as nondescript of a name as the two guys who'd taken me for a ride. The address was in Wichita on Waverly, a residential section of tract homes built in the late forties and early fifties. Pillbox houses. Small, square and all identical unless they'd been added on to and this one hadn't.

I was about a half a block up the street, partially obscured by a large bush, but where I could see the tan four door in the driveway. The neighborhood was, well, for lack of a better word, nice. Middle-America nice. Lawns were manicured, trees and bushes trimmed neatly, and flowerbeds bright and cheerful in the late afternoon sun. Waverly was tree-lined on either side with towering old pin oaks and sycamores.

Smithson's house was painted a neutral color with a lightly contrasting trim. A pink flowering Rose of Sharon bloomed at one end of the small porch and a bed of Black-eyed Susans spread out in front. Multi-colored Impatiens ringed the two trees in the yard. I think I even caught a whiff of Jasmine. Gosh, it was nice.

I got bored, ate a half a bologna and mustard sandwich. I don't do fancy when I'm on a stakeout. I checked my watch and fought off dozing. Finally, I got a bite. My rod jiggled and if I had a bobber, it would have jumped in the water. John Smithson walked out on the porch. I should have given odds and taken bets on which Sandy it would be. It was Light Sandy, followed by a woman in a light print cotton dress. Her hair was coifed, she sported an apron and although it was difficult to tell from where I was, I swear she had on a string of pearls. She kissed him on the cheek.

Goodbye honey. Do you expect a tough day at the office?

No. I just have to kill a couple of people. Should be home by dinner.

It looked like June Cleaver sending Ward off to work. I half-expected The Beaver or Wally to come bounding out with Lumpy or Eddie Haskell.

He looked to make sure she'd reentered the house and then he checked to verify the presence of his gun. He had a shoulder holster now. Then the chase was on. I followed him downtown and by the time we reached an old industrial area, I had to turn my lights on as evening settled in fast. He turned off of Waterman onto Commerce and I had to wait until he was far down the dead-end street before I could turn, and I cut my lights when I did.

Commerce is a bumpy brick-paved street of old warehouses, some functioning, some abandoned and some turned into upscale shops for antiques, art and fiber creations. On Friday and Saturday nights this portion of the street is packed with either those who want to be seen or those who want free wine and cheese at the gallery showings. It was dark and empty tonight.

I passed the closed-up shops and came to the dead-end part of the street where Smithson's car sat parked with three others outside of an abandoned brick-front warehouse with various old signs of the tenants down through the years. Proctors Coil and Springs, Blocks Lubrication, Santanas Central Card Stock. Geeze, nobody believes in possessive punctuation anymore.

An abandoned warehouse. If it could only be this easy. If that's where they had Janie, I might even consider calling Charlie and having her let loose the dogs of WPD to surround the place and smoke them out. Might. First things first.

I parked down a narrow alley, but backed in, just in case, and then went to a side door. It was unlocked and led past a short hallway of large-windowed offices that had cement floors and high ceilings. They had no furniture and were littered with paper and old boxes. Fixtureless wires hung from the ceiling. The hallway opened into the warehouse part, also empty, and I saw a light on the far side in a room at the top of a wooden stairway. If I could verify Janie's presence, then I'd deal with my ethical dilemma, to call or not to call.

I treaded lightly, but my steps echoed when I crossed the warehouse floor toward the stairway. Faint music came from the room at the top, so I hoped it masked my steps. At the top, I balanced myself on a stair step and chanced a peek through the large window. Five men, four playing cards with money on the table and Smithson's back to me, and who I presumed to be his brother, Dark Sandy, in the game. All had shoulder holsters on, with weapons. Bland rock came from a clock radio.

I scanned the room. Square. No windows, no other doors. No Janie. Damn.

"Bullshit. You didn't have them two aces at the beginning of this hand."

Dark Sandy raked in a pile of bills.

"Let's go Jamie," said Smithson, and Dark Sandy rose.

Hmmm. John and Jamie Smithson. How quaint. While Dark Jamie pocketed his winnings against protests of cheating, Light John turned and I did a quick slide down below window's edge, but I heard their steps already coming toward the door.

I bolted and slipped, and then slid down four steps on my tailbone before I could stop my fall. The door was opening ten feet above me, so I took the remaining stairs in two awkward leaps and then executed the only maneuver available to me. I flung my body down a dark hallway instead of onto the open warehouse floor.

The wooden stairs thundered as all five men descended, three of them shouting profanities at Dark Jamie. They stood yelling at the head of my hallway as the brothers Smithson walked across the warehouse toward the front entrance.

Shit. If they got away, I'd lose all hope of tracing Janie. But the yellers of profanity blocked my exit. I retreated down the dark hallway to the end, where a metal door was chained shut from the inside. I made a mental note to call OSHA when I had time.

A window ran across the top of the door. I heard car engine noise out front. Shit, again. A two-by-four lay on the floor. I picked it up and smashed the window out.

"What the hell is that?" The boys at the other end of the dark hall.

I reamed the glass shards out of the bottom of the window with the board and chinned myself up. I'd missed one shard and it cut into the palm of my left hand.

"I think it came from down there."

I heard their footsteps running the hall, toward me, as I flipped my torso over and through the opening, hit the ground hard on the outside and ran like hell. The locked door behind me rattled and profanities began anew.

I grabbed a cloth from behind my driver's seat, wrapped it around my bleeding hand, floored my truck and was out the alley and down the bricks of Commerce in a flash.

32

I'd lost them.

At Waterman I felt the bloodstone turtle in my pocket and decided. Right. Fifty-fifty, but turn right. Fortune smiled. They sat at the stoplight at Waterman and Washington waiting for the green, and it's a good thing, because this turned out to be a short journey. I never would have found them.

Within a few minutes and several turns, they pulled up in front of an airplane house on the edge of the industrial district, where old houses from the twenties, thirties and forties mingled with machine shops and warehouses and buildings both occupied and deserted.

I cut my lights, coasted on by and parked. I crouched low, unwrapped the bloody cloth and shined a penlight on my hand. It hurt like crazy. The cut wasn't deep, but it wouldn't stop bleeding. I took the tweezers out of a first aid kit I carry and pulled the one sliver of glass out of my palm, poured some antiseptic on it and cut a butterfly bandage. That seemed to stop the bleeding, but it still hurt.

My Ruger was secured in a shoulder holster and I put a Baby Eagle semiautomatic around my waist, plus I had my dirk in a waist sheath, too. Sometimes I felt stupid calling it a dirk, but there was something romantic about having a knife with a medieval name at hand, even if it was basically useless. It gave me a Prince Valiant sense of power.

The airplane house sat between an old vacant pet shop on one side and a tool and die machine shop on the other. An alley ran behind it with a brick warehouse that had no windows fronting the alley all along the back. Basically, they were isolated within the inner city. Good choice for a hostage, if this was where Janie was being kept.

I went up the alley from behind and looked at either side of the house. Vegetation, basically dead, but thick and overgrown, crowded each side. If Janie was inside, they had all fronts pretty well covered. If they were smart, they had her upstairs in the rear-end of the airplane, the horizontal, elevated tail part of the house.

They weren't smart. When I looked in through a window in the back, a heavyset African American man sat in the kitchen, back to me, staring off into the wild blue yonder, bored to death. Polynesian, Hispanic, white bread and now Black. Young, old, male, female. I admired this organization. They were an equal opportunity employer, and they didn't care whom they used or wasted.

And there she was. Janie sat in a chair opposite him, facing the window. I winked at her. She squinted at me for a moment and then winked back. Her guard looked at her and she scratched the eye she winked with.

I sidestepped and tried the back door. It was locked.

She'd seen me through the rear window, acknowledged it, and then masked it with her eye scratch. What a girl. I heard voices further inside and needed to assess how many before I tried anything. On one side of the house, through some thinner portions of the dead vines and bushes, I saw the Sandies Dark and Light sitting in arm chairs smoking and talking with Sua-Lua, who tried to gesture with both his good and bad hands. It wasn't going well. Two Hispanics sat on a couch watching TV. Six total, each with a sidearm.

All of a sudden Sandy Dark got up and he and Sua-Lua walked out the front door, down the steps and away. Four total. The odds were getting better.

Around at the back, I watched as the big guy got up, looked over his shoulder at Janie, took an ice pick and broke up some crushed ice in a bucket. He put a handful in a rock's glass and poured himself three fingers of bourbon, straight, sat down and started sipping, his back to the window but eyes on Janie.

"I'm thirsty." Janie got him to get up and get her a drink of water, and when his back was turned, she came to the window and undid the latch, but she couldn't lift the old, frozen sash.

"Here you go, kid." The guard handed her a glass of water and Janie turned abruptly with her back to the window. I slid down.

"Get back over here, sit down and stay put."

I peeked. He walked across a hall to a john to take a leak. Janie ran to the window and tried to open it, to no avail. I was about ready to bust it out, á la the warehouse incident, when winkie-tinks came out of the bathroom. He couldn't have spent more than ten seconds in there. He must have a bladder the size of a peanut.

Janie didn't hesitate. She grabbed the ice pick out of the bucket and thrust it up to the hilt in the guy's thigh. He screamed, grabbed his leg and fell backwards. I hit the sash hard from the outside, rattled the pane and knocked the sash loose from its moorings. Janie finally managed to throw open the window, but the wounded guard stood up, pulled the ice pick out of his leg and hopped to the window with blood streaming down his thigh.

Janie was half way through the window and had a hold of my hands when the Black guy grabbed her ankles from the inside. She screamed. By now, the others inside ran to the kitchen. One came out the back, rounded the corner and started firing.

I let go of Janie's hands, pulled my Ruger out and returned fire. Pop, pop, and the guy fell back into a half-dead rhododendron bush. When I looked back through the window, the room was empty except for the wounded guard whom they left to fend for himself. He staggered to one knee, pulled his nine and pointed. I let loose with one round to his chest and then ran to the front.

The four door and one of the other cars were gone, and Janie with them. I went around back. One of the Hispanics lay dead in the bushes. Inside, the guard was still breathing. I called 911, and sat down.

This was the first person I'd killed since I'd been a police officer. That was seven years ago when I took out a dealer in a crack house who came out of a bedroom firing at my partner. I didn't like it then and I didn't like it now. Still…

I counted my options and felt the cord knot up in my neck. Stay, and spend the next several hours answering questions. Call Charlie and explain. Leave. I had nowhere to go. This time I'd lost them for good. I heard the sirens.

I left.

33

Okay, I'd seen teenagers do this. It can't be that hard.

I tried text messaging Laura and driving at the same time. No go. I kept veering off and almost jumped the curb once, so I parked in a convenience store lot and executed the phone maneuver, verifying it was alright to call, and then punched in her number.

"Any action?" she answered.

"Not much," I said. "I killed one guy and maybe a second. Found Janie and lost her. That's about it." Silence. Count of five.

"You call Charlie?"

"No."

"O'Reilly, how can you do this?" Silence on my part. "What about Janie?"

"She was fine when I saw her, but I've completely lost them. I don't know where to go next." The cords in my neck knotted and I thought it would take a massage therapist with the weight of a Mastodon to release them. "What about you?"

"Nothing happening, but I got a lead on crack being available at a club on 21st Street later tonight." Silence. "Keep in touch O'Reilly. Don't change. But consider the advantages of contacting Charlie. Bye."

Don't change. What a kidder. But she was right about Charlie. I headed back to the airplane house to see if Charlie was on the call, but about halfway there, my phone rang. Actually it jingled. I tried answering it but had to pull over.

"You got action already?" I answered.

Silence. "You have made a big mistake, Mr. O'Reilly." It was the voice of Roderiguez.

"Where is she?"

"The question you should be asking is, is she still alive?"

"You didn't?" I said.

"You did not play by the rules, so I am changing the rules. You no longer have twenty four hours to make the arrangements. We make the arrangements now if I am not to kill the girl."

"Alright," I said. "We'll meet tomorrow at high noon on the main street of Cow Town." Cow Town is a tourist theme park near downtown Wichita.

He laughed. "High noon? Main Street? This is not the Old West, Mr. O'Reilly. No. We will meet at four tomorrow morning-"

"I can't get the transceiver by then."

"That is your problem. Four a.m. on the footbridge over the Big Arkansas at the Keeper of the Plains. I bring the girl to the middle, you bring the equipment to the middle. We exchange. I enter from the south. You enter from the north. Alone. Bring no one."

"And likewise for you. Alone, except for Janie," I said.

"Most certainly."

"Wait. You promised verification."

"Considering what has occurred earlier, I am sure you have seen the girl."

"I want to hear her voice and know she is still okay." I flexed my jaw and rotated my neck.

There was a silence, and then, "Mr. 'O,' is that you Mr. 'O'?

"Janie, are you alright?"

The phone went dead.

At least I'd established one thing. Janie was in the presence of Roderiguez now. They were at the same location. Whether both or neither of them showed at the bridge, the trail had been established.

What Roderiguez was advocating was suicide. For me. The Keeper of the Plains Statue stands forty-four feet high and is on top of a thirty foot man-made rocky promontory at the confluence of the Little and Big Arkansas Rivers. Footbridges span both rivers to the peninsula where the statue stands on sacred Indian ground. Alone in the middle of either bridge, I would be dead meat and easy pickings for a sniper. This didn't bode well.

Uniforms and plain-clothes were all over the airplane house. I could see Charlie on the porch talking with a reporter. I parked across the street, walked up and waited until she'd finished.

"You got a police band in your car, O'Reilly?"

"We got to talk, Charlie."

"Uh-oh. You're not going to tell me you got something to do with this?"

"Charlie-" I sat down on the step and told her the basics, but not all the details, like the set-up for the Keeper of the Plains meeting. "Are they both dead?" I asked.

"Yes, and the third one's in bad shape."

"Third one? There were only two. The Hispanic by the bush back there and the African American."

"The Black guy's not dead. He should make it. They just hauled him off. There's a third one, though." She walked me down past where I'd parked earlier and a tech was working over a body in the bushes. "You know him?"

"Sandy Dark. Jamie Smithson." I said. This was really getting puzzling.

"Come on downtown and we'll do a statement," she said.

"Unh-unh."

"What do mean, unh-unh? I can arrest you right now."

"I need time, Charlie. Janie's life is on the line."

"We'll take care of it. Give me the details and we'll get on it now."

"No. If I don't do this to the letter, she's dead. You have the best intentions, but I know how it goes down in the bureaucracy. I'm taking no chances."

"Then let's go." She pulled cuffs out. I think she was serious.

"Give me twelve hours. Twelve. That's all I'm asking. This is for Janie."

She looked off and I saw her soften. "Twelve and you come in. Period."

"Deal."

"By the bye, O'Reilly. Great meal, Saturday night," she said. "But it was kind of like Chinese. I'm still hungry."

Geeze. Another kidder.

34

"What happened to your hand, O'Reilly?"

Laura and I stood outside a club with no name in a strip mall on 21st Street.

"I had a disagreement with a window." I said.

"Looks like the window had better arguments."

"No," I said. "It'll never see the light of day again."

She called after I left the airplane house and said the action was on, and I'd told her about the exchange set up at the Keeper statue for four in the morning.

"I do want you to know, I've made contact with Charlie. She's given me twelve hours. Period."

Laura made little applause sounds with the fingertips of her hands.

"So what's happening, Laura?"

"Thrash and Phil entered the premises about twenty minutes ago, presumably to peddle their merchandise."

The strip mall consisted of storefronts that were empty or boarded up, except for the one with the no-name club. It had a Colt-45 Malt Liquor neon sign glowing in the door glass, and the wide, plate glass window was curtained so no one could see in. Bass vibrations shook the windows.

"Thrash and Phil at a Banger joint? Doesn't make sense."

"I'd say the Gang Bangers have set aside party loyalty tonight. I've seen everything come and go, from Black, Hispanic, Asian, White, you name it. Our two principles were escorted in, apparently with the blessing of the Banger management."

"Okay," I said. "Let's go sit down and set some rules of engagement." We each ate a sandwich in my truck where I'd parked across the street and where we had clear sight lines to the club, and talked it over. The bologna had gotten rubbery, but I ate mine anyway.

"We've got several hours before the Keeper exchange, so we can stay with this duo for awhile to see if they take us anywhere," I said. "But, what really bothers me is the logistics at the Keeper. I'll be on a ten foot wide cable suspended bridge, alone, in the middle of its three hundred and twenty foot length. Easy pickings for anybody from just about anywhere."

"You think Roderiguez himself will show at the Keeper?"

"No."

"You think he will actually send Janie with his second for the exchange?"

"No."

"Do you think he has any intention of letting you or Janie live once he's in possession of his electronics?"

"No, again."

"Then what's the purpose of going through with it?"

Unless the Miller crew leads us to Janie first, it's the only way of smoking somebody out to follow. Be thinking of a plan."

"The gears are already meshing, O'Reilly. Just be glad you've partnered with an incredible genius who is well-organized and willing to put aside her sense of fashion for one evening."

"I think you look dazzling tonight, even for a well-organized genius. I'm going in to take a look-see. Ring me up if anything breaks out here."

"In there? You'll stick out like a sore thumb."

She walked back over to the parking lot while I rummaged around in the back of my truck cab and pulled out a camouflage coat, put it on and turned up the collar. Then I found an old moth-eaten watch cap under the seat, which is what I call a Bronson cap after the motorcycle T.V. show from the seventies. Back then, I fancied myself a Michael Parks' clone and thought I would ride a Harley into the sunset, so I guess I've always kept a Bronson cap around as a memorial to those lost dreams.

The knit on my old cap was heavier that the modern Eminem type, but I rolled it down tight over the crown of my head, past my ears, affected the slouchiest saunter I was capable of, and then headed for the door. Laura just shook her head when I shuffled by.

Inside the front door a broad-shouldered Brother said, "Five dollar cover, man."

"I'm jamming tonight. Doing vocals for the band later." And then I added, "man." He didn't say anything as I walked on by without paying. The place was packed, smoke hung heavy and a steady bass beat boomed out of speakers and vibrated the whole room. I almost gagged as it was already rank with sweat and the smell of reefer. A twenty-something Hispanic girl offered me a joint, clung on my shoulder, and I had to literally push her off and find a spot against the wall where I could buy a twenty-two ounce plastic cup of draught beer so flat you couldn't flog a head into it. I leaned against the wall and clutched the plastic cup in one hand. I started sweating under my watch cap. How did the Eminem posers stand it?

Phil, sans uniform, weaved through the crowd on the other side of the room, dealing out of a coat pocket. Black, White, Brown, you name it, every color under the rainbow came up to him, slipped him the money, he handed the baggie back and off they went to Never-Never Land. It wasn't small change. It looked like he was handing out eight-ball packets. That must be two to three hundred at a minimum. Business was good. Roderiguez would be happy. Thrash worked another section of the room.

My cell jingled. "Hello." I was fast. I was starting to get the hang of the thing.

"We've got incoming." Laura's voice. "Two African Americans in a white Caddy just drove in along with Clare and Larry."

"Clare and Larry? How sweet. The hubby and the little woman are back together."

"Looks more like this is strictly business. That, or she's just keeping his pea-brain in line so he doesn't blow it."

The foursome walked through the door, Clare and Larry dressed as unobtrusively as possible and the two guys in full costume. Baggy, sagging pants with underwear protruding out the top, black tee-shirts with overlays of heavy silver chains and large medallions, Oakland raider caps with the bill set askew and off to one side.

I thought my slouchy saunter was better than theirs, but one of them smiled at somebody and flashed his grillz encrusted teeth. Talk about heavy metal. I couldn't match that if I had a Monex account.

The smoke was getting to my sinuses and eyes. I headed back out to Laura, but got stopped at the door.

"You said you playing. When you playing, man?" The bouncer was after me again. The man was relentless.

"I developed a bad case of laryngitis," I said, straining my voice. "I got to go. Sorry." And I headed for the door, but he stepped in front of me, blocking my path.

"You owe me five," and he held out a giant hand, size fourteen if it would have been a shoe. "Cover charge, dude. Remember?"

I looked around and decided it wasn't worth a gamble, so I took five ones out and handed them over. He parted like the Red Sea, and I shot out the door before you could say "Daddy Rabbit," not bothering to get my hand stamped.

Out in the lot people milled around, smoking and talking, with the bass rattling the windows and my chest.

"Couldn't take it anymore," I said to Laura.

"Pansy." She winced. "You smell like a humidor."

A cell phone went off. "Yours or mine?" I said. Oh God, I was becoming a monster. I sounded like all the other people in restaurants and elevators.

"Hello," I said.

"I got something you want. We need to meet."

"I know. I'll see you at four at the Keeper statue." Except it wasn't Roderiguez, it was the raspy croak of Sua-Lua's.

"I got something else. You're gonna need the transceiver. Come and get it."

I laughed. "Yeah, sure Sua-Lua. What the hell you talking about?"

"Like I said. I got it. You need it. We gonna meet."

"You haven't got Jack Shit."

"Look under your dash," he said.

I panicked. I walked across the street and popped open the cutaway in my truck. The transceiver was gone. "How in the hell did you get your hands on that?" I said.

"Never mind. You and me gonna meet. One hour. Chisholm Creek Park on the North Oliver side."

"Park's closed after dark."

"Jump the gate," he said.

I walked back to Laura. "Complication. Somehow, Sua-Lua got a hold of the transceiver."

"I thought you hid it in that secret compartment in your truck."

"I did, but it's gone and that was him demanding I meet him, now. The only thing I can figure is… I don't know. He and Jamie Smithson left the airplane house together. Smithson's dead. Smithson might have seen me reach for the button when he and his brother picked me up and then put two and two together after the fact. Who knows? I've got to get out to Chisholm Creek Park. Let's meet-"

"Think about it O'Reilly. Why's he doing this? Why doesn't he just turn the thing over to Roderiguez and claim his reward?"

"Revenge?"

"Exactly. He wants to take you down himself. Ask yourself, what do you need the transceiver for? It's all a bluff anyway."

"Right, as usual. I'd still feel better if I had it in my hands."

Our conversation was cut short. Clare and Thrash, along with the two Bangers, exited the club.

"As the world turns, our lovers are back together," I said. "Okay, I stand-up the Islander and go with these guys while you keep this flank covered. If our paths don't cross again, we meet at the Keeper at three to set up our defense. I'm counting on your genius for the plan."

35

A dirt alley bisected the length of the block, with short back yards on either side of it, each with an old one or one-and-a-half story house situated on it. The Caddy parked next to Clare's Denali, a quarter of the way down the alley, and I could see them get out and walk through a chain link fence gate. I parked on the side street and walked the alley up to the gate.

Tupac rap blared from somewhere inside the house, it was one of the extra half-story variety. I went to the quiet side and entered a screened-in porch, where I sidled up next to a closed and curtained door. Four of them. One of me. I only needed Clare. If I could isolate her, get her out and then offer her a choice. Take me to Roderiguez or be turned over to WPD.

The curtain hung on the inside of the door, but it gapped a little in the center, and I could see Clare counting stacks of money on a coffee table. She concentrated hard on the task and kept a running tally. I didn't have a view of the whole room, but she looked to be alone. I tried the door handle and it turned, so I drew the Ruger, softly opened the door and walked in. This needed to be quick.

"Let's go Clare. You're coming with me," I said just loud enough to be heard over the music. I leveled the Ruger at her.

She hid her surprise and stayed calm, flicked her black hair back over her shoulders and then opened her mouth as if to call out to the others.

"Don't do it, Clare. I won't hesitate." I moved the revolver forward for emphasis.

She thought better of it and kept her eye on me, but she glanced to the edge of the table at an automatic. Then she started gathering up the money.

"Leave it and don't touch the piece either. Walk toward me and as I back up, go out the door and on to the porch. I'll follow, gun trained on your back the whole time."

She rose, took a step and then two shots rang out. I dove across the room, hit the floor, rolled into the next room and came up to crouch position, aiming the Ruger through the door. I had no idea where the shots came from, but someone turned the music off from above and I heard footsteps come down the stairs from the half-story part of the house, and then Thrash's voice.

"They're taken care of, Babe. Grab the money and let's blow this place. Hey, where are you?"

I heard the Denali start up outside in the alley.

I came around the corner, gun up, but Thrash rounded the base of the stairs, a nine still in his hand and he turned on me and raised the gun. I took him down with one shot. A good portion of the money was gone from the table, along with the automatic. By the time I went through the screened-in porch and into the back yard, Clare and her Denali were gone, the engine noise fading in the distance.

I checked Thrash. He was dead. Upstairs, the two Bangers had taken one shot each to the head from Thrash's nine.

I sat on the couch downstairs and looked at Thrash's body. He was now the second person I'd killed since I was a police officer and I was liking it even less. I thought about my dream. There had been no truth to it, and my wife's advice betrayed me. She was wrong. There was no abiding peace and violence only followed me everywhere I went. There would be no escape from the O'Reilly legacy.

I might as well face Sua-Lua whether I needed the transceiver or not, and be done with it. That seemed to be the way of things.

I called it in, walked the alley to my truck and drove to North Oliver.

36

I jumped the gate at Chisholm Creek Park and walked the winding quarter mile back in to the picnic pavilion. He might have been hiding anywhere in the brush and taken me with one shot, but I didn't think that's what he really wanted. I was right.

When I got to the pavilion, the transceiver lay on a picnic table in the center of the open-air structure. I walked the perimeter and then a little way down the footpath. He didn't jump out at me or come running up the path swinging some primitive jungle weapon over his head. That was a relief. He surely wasn't going to let me walk away with it though. Maybe he was waiting to take me from behind on my return trip.

I stepped up on the cement pad of the pavilion and walked to the center table. Maybe the transceiver or the table was rigged with explosives. I started to bend over to examine it when my peripheral vision picked up the movement, but it was too late.

He came from above, out of the fretwork of beams in the open A-framed roof. He dropped behind me, and I whirled around and stumbled back against a fifty-five gallon trash can, knocking it over. It clattered on the cement floor until it rolled to a stop.

His squat body stood there looking like a fat thumb, and he had a wild glare in his eyes.

"Kill any mosquitoes lately?" I said.

"No. Only Palangi." His voice had more gravel in it than I remembered.

"What's that?"

"Palangi. That means White Guy. You are the next Palangi to die."

"Yikes. A racist Polynesian. I heard that's more dangerous than a wounded rhino." I stared at a sword he held. He really did have a primitive jungle weapon.

"You like?" he said. "My nifo oti. My warrior hacking sword."

Its wooden handle had what looked like sharks teeth imbedded in one end, while the other end terminated in a metal hook that had a piece of cloth attached. It had been soaked in something and smelled like naphtha. I stood up and he produced a striking match in his cast hand, ran it across the cement, and lit the cloth on his blade.

"Oooh, a vorpal blade," I said. "Does it go snicker-snack?"

He whipped it through the air and started twirling it.

Yes, it does, I said to myself. "Look, I said I was sorry about the wrist. You don't accept apologies, or what?"

Then he began doing some intricate ceremonial foot stomping routine.

"You know in the NFL, they penalize you fifteen yards on the kickoff for that sort of behavior." I braced myself for a charge at any moment, although I wasn't sure what I was going to do. Then it came.

He rolled his flaming knife around his neck as preparatory for a strike and then he came at me, screaming. I thought about an end-around, but settled on a simple fake left, motion right, as I jumped up on the picnic table and the weight of his sword carried him on through and it imbedded itself in a wooden support post. By the time he'd freed the thing, I'd gotten my balance and pulled the Ruger out.

Give the guy credit. He was fast and agile for a fat man with a broken wrist. The fire was dying, but the flat of the blade came around and knocked the gun from my hand. He raised the blade for a hack, but I threw a right cross into his gut and it made him drop the sword. I kicked it to the edge of the cement pad, swung around and brought both arms down and across his shoulder blade. He staggered, but he came up under me, pushing me back like a defensive tackle, until I slammed into a support post and he pinned me against it.

Then he let loose with a punch from his good hand like a Titan missile leaving a silo, right into the center of my solar plexus. The wind went out of me and he threw another one, higher, and I felt a rib snap and pain shot across my chest. He rolled across the floor to the sword, picked it up and charged me again, but I pulled my dirk from its sheath and gave it a quick flick. It sunk deep into his shoulder. He dropped like a sack of pineapples.

"You must've skipped school the day they gave the lesson on jungle maneuvers with small knives," I said.

He looked at the imbedded knife, stunned, and then passed out.

I didn't bother to pull it out. "Keep it as a souvenir," I said.

I picked up the Ruger and the transceiver, and then started a trot back to the gate, but stopped short with the rib pain in my side. It would be slow going and I didn't know if I'd make the meeting time with Laura at the Keeper.

37

The red 'Vette sat alone in the dark north lot. Laura wasn't there.

I grabbed the transceiver, and then checked the chambers of my Ruger securing it in my pocket holster. I shoulder-holstered the 9 mm Baby Eagle and winced when a pain shot up my side. Sua-Lua's rib-work on me had taken its toll. Then I brought out the Remington M 24 with an MK 440 night scope, put on a light jacket and a Royal's baseball cap and then walked over the shorter bridge, across the Little Arkansas to the peninsula where the Keeper statue stood. The forty-four foot tall Cor-Ten steel Indian, arms raised to the sky, towered above the confluence, and a steady pounding sounded out from water as it flowed over the dam on the Little's side.

Laura sat cross-legged on the flagstones, her equipment spread around her as she checked it.

"How's tricks?" she said.

I told her about Clare, Thrash and the two Bangers. "Oh, and I got to flick my dirk. I can't believe I actually got to use it."

"I can't believe you actually said that. Flick your dirk? Why don't you call it what it is, O'Reilly? It's a knife, for God-sakes."

"Knife, dirk, whatever, the last I saw it, it was sticking in Sua-Lua's shoulder."

"We agreed you weren't going to meet."

"Well, I had a little extra time on my hands. One thing led to another."

She just shook her head.

"So, what's the game-plan, oh great genius?"

She rose and we walked up to the bridge that spanned the Big Arkansas as she explained. The bridge itself is a cable-stay suspended expanse, three hundred and twenty feet long. It's ten feet wide with a handrail and steel cable strung along each side, but otherwise, it's open to the murky flow thirty or forty feet below, depending on the river's water level.

I looked around. Nobody else was out and about.

"You'll go to the center as planned, to meet Roderiguez or whomever he sends," she said.

I looked down the peninsula's edge at the rugged vegetation, and the across the river on the other side at the manicured walkers' path. The lamplight was minimal, but enough to see well up close and make out shapes in the distance.

"That leaves me rather exposed, wouldn't you say?"

"Yep."

"He might hide a sniper in the brush down there, or put one in the open on the other side," I said.

"There could already be one in the brush for all we know. That's where the genius comes in," she said. "I'll be up there."

We looked up to the top of the thirty-foot rocky promontory the giant statue stood on top of.

"I'll have a clear field of vision, three hundred and sixty degrees, and can take all comers with your Remington and the night scope. That's nice hardware, O'Reilly."

"You still have your underwear imprinted with the Marksman crossed rifles emblem?" It was a legend from the old days that Laura had emblazoned her personals with the emblem after she attained Marksman status.

I got the deadpan stare, then, "I've kept up O'Reilly. Don't worry, your butt's covered as well as mine. We'll wear the two-way and be in constant communication."

"Great plan. I love it, with one exception. How's about you put on my ball cap and jacket, walk out there fully exposed, and I go up top?"

"I never expose myself in public," she said. "Now, come help me."

We imbedded pitons in the rock face, and set up carabiners and nylon rope.

"What's wrong?" Laura saw me wince when I raised my arm with a piton in hand.

"I think Sua-Lua cracked a rib."

Laura climbed to the top of the promontory. "Great view," she said.

"Wish I was there."

We donned our two-way gear and checked communication.

"Okay O'Reilly, now we wait." She called down to me from the edge. "And I want you to realize something. Assuming he doesn't bring Janie, we need somebody out of this. If we don't take someone at least half-alive, we have no road to Janie. This is her last hope."

"I've thought of that too," I said. It was a grim thought.

"Go to the edge of the bridge, but stay back and behind the wall until you hear from me, and wait."

I did. We waited. Twenty minutes, then my headset crackled.

"It's ten past four. This had better not be for nothing, O'Reilly."

"If it is…" But I trailed off, thinking of Janie's fate. Another five minutes passed, and then, radio noise.

"Be alert," she said. "They're approaching. One car in the Exploration Place lot across the river. They're cruising the perimeter. They've stopped at the steps leading down to the bridge."

"You got numbers?"

"Not yet. They're still in the car."

Another two minutes went by. "Show yourself, O'Reilly."

I stepped out and onto the edge of the bridge and stopped. My hand went into my pocket and stayed on the Ruger. I could see car doors opening and figures getting out. "What do we have?"

"We got us four total. Two are coming down the steps. One short. Maybe Janie. It's her build anyway. The other taller. No visible weapons. The two at the car have long guns, probably semis. All the doors are open, nobody left in the car."

I could see the tall and short figure at the bottom of the steps as they approached the far side of the bridge and then stopped.

"Okay, O'Reilly. It's show time. Do your thing and do it good."

"Likewise, I'm sure." I started walking slowly toward the center of the bridge, as did the two-some on the other side. About a third of the way out, Laura reported in on the headset.

"It's not Janie."

"Surprise, surprise," I said.

"The shorter one is a male in his twenties, but a look-alike for Janie's stature. The big one's not Hispanic, so it's not Roderiguez."

I slowed my gait a little. "Who takes whom?"

"Whom? I always did admire your fine use of English grammar, O'Reilly."

"I'm running short of time out here."

"I'm going back to the two on the far side. You deal with Mutt and Jeff. Good luck."

I was on my own standing twenty feet from the duo. They kept walking and stopped about ten feet from me.

"I come for Mr. Roderiguez piece of equipment." This from the tall one. He was big and looked well-muscled. He could probably hold his own.

"He was supposed to come himself."

"He couldn't make it."

"He was supposed to send the girl."

"She's in the car."

"I don't think so," I said.

"Hand it over." The big one did all the talking.

"What if I don't want to?" This sounded like conversation I had in the third grade on the playground.

"What other choice do you have?" he said.

"Let's see, I choose... you come with me and take me to the girl, and then I produce the equipment."

He laughed. "Hey Joel, this guy's funny, isn't he? A real comedian."

The little guy didn't laugh. I guess Joel didn't think I was funny.

"Okay, we'll do it the hard way." Big guy pulled back his jacket and started to take a piece out of a waist holster.

"Guns drawn," I said to Laura into my two-way, and I let loose with one shot from the Ruger inside my pocket. The big guy went down, and as he reached for his dropped gun, I kicked it over the edge. But Joel was on me, trying to take me down.

"What's the matter, Joel?" I said. "You too little for a cap pistol? Maybe they'll give you one for Christmas."

I heard a loud report from on top of the promontory, and then in my headset, Laura said, "one's down at the car, the second one's retreated behind it," and I heard an exchange of fire.

Joel was tougher than I thought he would be for a little guy, but I came up under him, flipped him off and away from me, and my ribcage felt like a sledge hammer hit it. When he charged, I sidestepped, grabbed his jacket and threw him forward against the rail. He went partway through the opening between steel cables, so I went after him hard, trying to pull him around and throw him into his partner. But he fought it, and when he pulled back I went into him and my weight shoved him on through the cables. I heard his scream and then the splash below.

The big guy was up on one knee, but floundering, when Laura reported again. The shots had stopped. "The other one's taken out," she said.

"Rappel yourself on down Rapunzel, and claim your spoils. I've got a live one on the bridge, as requested." I pulled the Ruger out and went to the big guy, whose left knee had been blown open by my one shot. He fell back over, rolling on one side and yelling about how much it hurt.

"Now I get to choose," I said to him. "Guess what it's going to be?"

Laura jogged on by me to the other side of the river, with a semiautomatic in hand, and was back a couple of minutes later. "They're both dead. What about the Janie impersonator?" she said.

"I don't know. It's a swift current. They'll find him downstream, but I doubt if he'll be alive." Number three, I thought to myself and shook my head. The carnage kept on coming.

"You okay?" said Laura.

"Yeah." It was a hollow empty yeah though. Then I thought of Janie. "Let's load the big guy up and get going," I said.

We left the climbing gear, but gathered up the firepower, and then between the two of us, prodded, dragged and carried our wounded captive to the north parking lot. It took awhile.

We wrapped his knee to minimize the bleeding and then unceremoniously dumped him in the cab space behind the seats in my truck.

"You drive," I said to Laura, "While I tend to the wounded." She looked at the dried stain of blood from my shoulder wound, climbed in and pulled out onto Central.

"What's your name?" I said to the big guy who was groaning in the back.

"Lucky," he moaned.

"Lucky? You gotta be kidding. Now it's my turn to laugh. Hey Laura, this guy's name is Lucky. Is this a working definition of irony, or what?"

"Now what'd you do that for?" she said. "You used my name. You said 'Laura'. Now we gotta kill him."

He yelled some profanity from the back, half rose up and threw a half-hearted, useless punch into the air.

"Oh, Lucky strikes" I said. "Naw Laura, we don't gotta do that. I can tell, he's too smart to talk. Hey Lucky. I bet you'd like some medical attention for that knee of yours." I was on my knees, reversed in the seat, looking over and down at him. The wrapping helped, but blood was still smearing on the floor.

"Yeah, get me to the hospital."

"We can do that, Lucky. But we got business to take care of first and as soon as we do, we'll race you to a hospital, Scout's honor." I held up three fingers but I don't think he saw them. "You can help out though. Where's the girl at?"

"I don't know."

"Where's Roderiguez?"

"Don't know."

"Okay," I said. "Let's play a little game. It's called 'Bad Knee, Good Knee,' and here's how it's played." I held my Ruger up so he could see me empty all the rounds and then I put one back in and spun the wheel.

"You have one bad knee, but you do still have one good one. It would be a shame if anything happened to it. Now tell me, where is Roderiguez and the girl?"

"I don't know."

"Then, let the game commence," I said. "Bad knee, good knee." I pointed the Ruger at his good knee and pulled the trigger. Click. Nothing.

"Ahhh, God," he screamed.

"Hmmm. Maybe you really are lucky, Lucky. Once again, where are they?"

"I tell you I don't know."

"There wasn't a bullet in that chamber, but do you want to take a chance on the next one? Odds are getting slimmer, Lucky."

"If I knew I'd tell you. You got to believe me."

"Okay then. Bad knee, good knee." I took aim.

"Alright, alright," he yelled, "put it away," and he gave us an address in College Hill.

"This had better be correct Lucky, because if it isn't, both knees will need medical attention and you won't even be able to be classified as part of the walking wounded."

Laura turned my truck and headed east toward College Hill, then glanced over at me and said "Bad Knee, Good Knee? Come on, O'Reilly."

38

"This is going to hurt a little."

Lucky groaned as I bound him with duct tape.

"Sorry," I said, and we gagged him and covered him with a tarp in the back of my cab. "I'll keep my promise about the medical attention, assuming your information is good."

College Hill is an old section of homes, its streets lined with towering oaks and ash trees. The houses come from the second quarter of the twentieth century, all expensive but some more so than others. They run the gamut from fairytale-like cottages with peaked fronts, like the one in the Hansel and Gretel storybook, to mid-sized Tudor two-stories, to near palatial estates.

The address Lucky had given us was one of the latter. It took up nearly an entire half of a square block. It was walled and gated on the sides and front, but we could see the massive, gray stone structure through the gate. Security cameras were mounted on the walls. Along the backside from the next street over, the grounds were protected with thick vegetation, both trees and brush. That's where we parked when we further incapacitated Lucky. We double-checked our firepower and Laura slid her Aikido staff down through her belt.

"Did you actually have a round chambered when you played your little knee game with Lucky?" she asked.

I smiled at her and shrugged. Then I looked at the thick and overgrown vegetation that obscured the backside of the grounds.

"I figured there might not be any security cameras on this side with all the brush," I said to Laura. We were parting limbs and branches, some with thorns, as we tried to make our way through it.

"Why don't you whistle," she said, "and see if Sua-Lua will come running? Maybe he's got a machete we can use."

It took a good twenty minutes to work our way through about ten yards of the stuff before we came out the other side. The back grounds were enormous. The first tinges of morning light came into the sky, and across the manicured expanse of lawn and flower beds and statues, the blue of a swimming pool glowed from its underwater lights. We skirted the perimeter, keeping to the darkest sections, until we stood in shadows and bushes opposite a garage, a two story affair with accommodations above the four cars housed below. Its gray stone exterior matched the house.

Larry Miller and Ex-Deputy Phil came out of the house and we watched them wind around and through several other cars parked outside the garage on a wide circle of concrete. Clare's Denali was among them. They walked inside the garage, and a minute later, lights went on above, in the second story quarters.

"Not much activity, considering what all Roderiguez has at stake right now," I said.

"There's got to be some muscle around here somewhere," she said. "He's not going to sit around with no protection."

Just then, two guys with semiautomatic rifles slung over their shoulders strolled around the corner on a path of pavers, smoking and chatting it up in muffled tones, unconcerned and oblivious to any threat. When they cut around the next corner, I motioned to Laura and we beat it across the flagstone skirt around the pool and entered the door Larry and Phil came out of, and walked into a mudroom.

"Okay," I said. "This is it. Let's give them one hundred and eight."

"You mean a hundred and ten? As in percent?"

"No. One-o-eight. That's how many stitches are in a baseball. Vernon Johnson once told me to keep them off-stride with your two-seamer. Just when they think they got your rising fastball figured out and are ready to pounce on it, give them the two-seamer and let the bottom drop out of it. It's time to let the bottom drop out on them."

We drew our Baby Eagles and walked through the mudroom that opened into a giant kitchen with a twelve foot ceiling, a center butcher block big enough you could gut a cow on it, and pots and pans hanging everywhere.

"Pretty fancy," Laura whispered. "You think he actually knows how to use all this stuff?"

"Maybe he watches the Food Channel."

The whole lower level was dark and quiet, and as we wound our way through it with firepower in hand, we found a labyrinth of halls, passages, rooms and dead-ends.

"I think we've been here before," I said.

"Yeah. We're going in circles."

When we came out in the front entryway, we looked up maybe twenty feet to the top where a landing stood for the stairway that descended to our feet. It looked like something right out of "Sunset Boulevard."

"Why don't you go stand up there, pose, and tell Mr. De Mille you're ready for your close-up," I said.

"Yeah, and maybe you'll wind up face down in the pool."

"So, where the hell is everybody?"

"You gotta think," she said, "he's expecting his boys back at any minute with the transceiver. Wouldn't he be a little anxious about that?"

We heard a door open and close upstairs. "Let's go," I said, and we climbed up, looked both ways and went far right toward the sound, standing on either side of a door with a thin line of light shining out from underneath it. And then, another sound deeper back in the upstairs' labyrinth.

"I'll take that one. This one's yours," she said, and went on down the hall toward the other sound.

I turned the doorknob and heard Clare's voice. "Is that you Phil?"

"No it's not, Clare. It's me again." I had the Ruger leveled at her. She had what money she made off with earlier, as well as whatever more Phil and Larry took in after she left the club, spread in front of her on a desk. A side drawer was open. She slumped back in her chair, hand sliding toward the drawer, as I moved in closer, standing in front of the desk. I could see the gun handle in the open drawer.

"Twice in one night," she said. "What an honor." She paused and stared at me. "Thrash?"

"He's dead," I said. "I didn't have any choice. He turned on me and raised and pointed his weapon."

"You son-of-a-bitch." She stared some more and seemed to be thinking through her possibilities. "You don't really have hopes of making it out of here alive, do you, Mr. O'Reilly?"

"Right now the only hope I have is for you to take me to Janie. Then I hope to turn you in to stand trial for the murder of Vernon Johnson."

"You're a fool, Mr. O'Reilly. Such a fool. You have no idea what a complete fool you are."

I started to make a crack about which fool was holding a gun, but I blinked and stood silent, thinking for a moment. Something clicked, and suddenly intuition merged with reason and it all came together for me. "You didn't kill him," I blurted out.

She just stared at me.

"You didn't kill Vernon Johnson, did you?"

"I never said I did."

It's odd how one word can mesh such disparate and unrelated events. Buford Thomas had used the same word. He'd said Vernon was an old fool who deserved to rot in his field until buzzards stripped him of his innards.

"You said before, that Vernon Johnson was a fool, that he had no idea, and you weren't just talking about Lael's murder when you said that, were you? He had no idea what all the meth paraphernalia was even if he did stumble across it, did he? He left your place alive and you did not kill him, I'll lay odds on it."

"What does it matter?"

"It matters to me."

"Like I said, you're a fool, just like him. I gave that old man one of the postcards from Nashville I'd faked to make Larry and everyone else think Lael had run off to find her fame and fortune. Phil was there. He told him Lael had been back for a visit and the old man believed it."

"Postcard? The Grand Ole Opry?" I said.

"What?"

I remembered the postcard of the Grand Ole Opry I'd seen in Buford Thomas' house.

I got a mental picture of Buford traipsing across his field to confront Vernon, a man he called a creature of routine and whose routine he knew well. He expected to find him back from his routine Saturday morning breakfast with Bob. When he wasn't there, Buford must have waited until he returned, getting hotter and hotter over the illegal water feud. When Vernon finally came back from his Good Samaritan attempt at the Millers, hot-headed Buford waited in the drive, preventing him from entering the pole barn. They faced off, he erupted and then claimed the postcard as a trophy.

"Why'd you go to Doc Smally and blackmail him to change cause of death?" I asked Clare.

She looked at me like I was an idiot. "Phil called and told me about Johnson. I knew those bones had to be somewhere on his land. An inquiry would have found them eventually and then questions would have been asked. I had to prevent that somehow."

"Oh, you did a great job of that."

"The hell with you." She reached for the open drawer, but I cuffed her across the head with my handgun. She went out, her head on the desk.

Laura came through the door. "I can't find anybody in this maze. What's with her?"

"She called me a fool."

"That's why I never use bad names with you," she said.

"Clare said something else, too, but I'll tell you later."

Out in the hall, we went the other way and reached the stairs just as Sua-Lua came to the top. We stood face to face, his eyes big with surprise. He had a bulky bandage under his shirt on the knifed shoulder. His good hand held a broad-bladed sword, not as wicked as the one from the pavilion, but definitely lethal.

"You come back for more?" His raspy voice grated on the air.

"You must have baling wire for vocal chords," I said, but he was already coming at us, his blade raised.

Laura dropped her gun, pulled out the Aikido staff and came down on his neck and bad shoulder all in one quick movement. He didn't have time to blink. His face looked like it had been hit with a taser and he fell for a second time in one night, out cold.

"You need to file a disability claim, Buddy." I said.

"I don't think he can hear you."

"Well, that's two down and out, and two that can't take us to Janie," I said.

"We're getting there."

We went left now and when we came to a split in the maze, Laura kept on to the left and I turned down a long hallway. I saw an open door at the end with lights on. Roderiguez sat looking at a computer screen, his back to the door.

I surveyed the room. It was large, with a second door, open on the other side near his desk and leading down still another hallway. There was a wet bar with various liquor bottles and glasses on it. Wood paneling decked out three sides of the room, and the fourth consisted of a row of leaded glass windows overlooking an interior courtyard below. An enormous stone fireplace, big enough you could walk into it, was in the far paneled wall.

I did a fairly good imitation of Sua-Lua's gravelly voice. "Lucky's back with the transceiver," I said, my 9 mm in hand.

"Excellent." He didn't turn around. "Bring it to me and then get rid of the girl."

"You sent the wrong boys for the job," I said in my own voice. He spun around in his chair and stood. "You should have taken care of it yourself, Roderiguez."

He didn't even blink. "I told you earlier on the phone that you made a big mistake. Now you have made two."

"Let's cut to the chase. Take me to Janie."

"That will never happen, Mr. O'Reilly."

"Your demonstration at the firing range was not wasted on me. I learned a lot. The problem is, my aim is not as good as yours. I don't always hit what I'm shooting at. Take for instance right now, I'm aiming at your computer screen." I pulled the trigger and sent one whizzing past his ear and into the wall. He didn't flinch. "Oops. I missed. Now, take me to Janie."

"Never."

"Let's see if I can hit the computer this time." I squeezed off a second round and clipped his ear this time. He grabbed his ear and fell back in the chair, blood trickling through his fingers.

"Mistake number three, Mr. O'Reilly."

At least I made him blink that time. But then, a large pair of arms came around me from the back, pinned my arms to my sides and squeezed the breath out of me with pain shooting through my ribs. My Baby Eagle clunked on the hardwood floor.

"Bring him closer, Johnny," said Roderiguez, who held a blood-soaked bar towel to his ear.

Johnny lifted me with his bear hug and brought me in closer while I gasped for breath. There was a second person next to him. Probably the two goons we'd seen walking the pavers.

"Manuel, go get the girl. We will dispose of them both at the same time. Johnny, search Mr. O'Reilly until you find my transceiver."

Johnny let loose and I gulped in oxygen. Then he turned a knob and gas jets ignited across the width of the giant fireplace. He picked up an iron poker and held it in the flames until it glowed, and then he touched it on the inside of my right thigh. My pants smoldered and I felt a searing pain spread across my upper leg as I buckled and dropped to my knees. There was a rancid smell of burnt flesh.

"I don't think it's there," said Johnny. "Maybe it's somewhere near his face." He lifted the poker next to my cheek and gave me a mean smile. I felt the heat pulsing off the poker as it wavered next to my face.

There was a whoosh sound as Laura's staff flew across the room from the other doorway, hit the poker and knocked it out of Johnny's hand. He sat stunned for a moment, and then crawled on his hands and knees toward my gun while Roderiguez went for Laura, thinking her slight build meant physical weakness. This was his mistake number one.

Laura had already planted her feet, centered herself and was extending her ki. When Roderiguez reached her, she executed a joint lock, countered his weight, stopping him cold, and took him down. He should have stayed there. Mistake number two. When he rose and came at her again, she moved off the line of attack, crossed her arms over in a Mountain Mist movement to hide her technique, and then used a rotation throw, the force of which sent his body flying across the room, crashing through the lead glass windows and landing on the flagstone courtyard below. We heard the crunch of bone and body over the sound of falling glass.

By that time I fought through the pain in my leg and chest and had toppled Johnny-The-Bear from behind, but he'd brushed me aside with one paw, picked up my Baby Eagle and fired at Laura as she turned from her body throw on Roderiguez. A red stain spread across her shirt from the right shoulder and down her side. She fell back against the fireplace and slid down.

By then, I'd picked up her staff, which I didn't know how to use, and I began beating the shit out of Johnny-The-Bear, knocking my gun away and driving him back to the wall.

"Stay down," I shouted to Laura, as she tried to rise up while I was flailing away. Johnny held his arms and hands to protect his face, and he kept trying to get up himself until I got inside and thwacked him across his head. I hit him so hard, I opened up the glass wound on my hand. I heard his jawbone split and tissue rip loose, and blood spurted out of a mangled nose as he finally went down for good.

"I said to stay down, Laura." But she was on her knees with her semiautomatic trained across the room at the door I had come through. Manuel stood there, his hands in the air and Janie next to him.

Janie screamed, ran to Laura and held her as Laura went limp and slid back down on the floor. I prodded Manuel with the staff over to the broken-out window so he could look down at his boss' body sprawled out below, and contemplate his own possible fate.

Then I called 911.

39

Hospitals are depressing places to spend any amount of time, so twice in one week was a bit too much for me.

Laura was in surgery, while Janie talked with a police woman first and then what they call a personal counselor. I'd talked with two different officers and now I sat on an examining table getting my ribs, cut hand and leg burn tended to by a young, gorgeous emergency room doctor who looked like she was still in her first year of med school. Ah, the perks of being in the crime business.

Charlie walked in while Doctor Sue, or whatever her name was, rubbed a soothing ointment on my thigh burn. Charlie watched for a minute and when Sweet Sue went to get the bandages, she said, "If you need someone to help you change your dressings, just let me know."

I smiled. I love attention.

"So, how's it going, Bruiser?" she asked.

"I'm still kicking."

"You know, O'Reilly-" She stopped and shook her head. "Lorna Doone, I don't even know what to say to you. I don't know where to begin. How's Laura?"

"In surgery. No updates yet."

Sue was back. "I'm going to start bandaging." She was beautiful, but her voice was sugary and cloying. She touched the burn. "Does that hurt?"

"Not when you do that." I said, in a high register. I probably couldn't stand her voice for more than a half an hour, though. Good rationale.

Charlie shook her head again. "It looks like the O'Reilly clan curse of violence has caught up with you again. How many did you personally waste on tonight's trail of blood?"

"The Hispanic at the airplane house and the Black guy if he didn't make it."

"No, he's okay. The ice pick wound will fester though."

"Good." I nodded. "Thrash at the drug house south of Twenty-First Street is number two. Then there's this guy named Joel floating somewhere downstream from the confluence."

Sue looked up at me from my thigh. I don't know if it was fear or admiration. I'm going with admiration.

"You mean there's one out there we don't know about yet?" Charlie said.

"That's it. Three total. I figure all the others will make it."

"You didn't kill Roderigeuz?"

"No, that was Laura's handiwork. Did you find Larry Miller and Phil?"

"They were hopped up on some of their own merchandise over the garage, oblivious to the gunshot, sirens and anything else in the real world. That Lucky character may walk again, someday, if he's lucky. Clare

Miller has a nasty cut and a bruise you gave her, but she'll be put away for a long time for two murders."

"Just one. She didn't kill Vernon Johnson."

Sue was giving us strange looks now. She finished up in a hurry and beat a hasty retreat, busying herself at a tray of stainless steel knives and whatchama-call-its. My admiration quota must have dropped significantly.

I explained it all to Charlie and she said, "Getting that to stand up in court good enough for a conviction on this Buford Thomas will be difficult, at best."

Before she left, I said, "As soon as my leg is well enough for action, I want you over for dinner."

"Been there. Done that."

"No. I mean just you and me this time."

"We'll need a statement from you, O'Reilly. Tomorrow sometime."

Later, I sat in the waiting room with Janie until we got word on Laura.

Janie cried and said, "She just has to make it. She can't die, she just can't."

"Don't worry," I said. "Laura's tougher than woodpecker lips."

That made her smile and she hugged me. I cherish that hug to this day.

When Laura was finally out of surgery and awake, they let us go into the recovery room, for just a minute. She lay there with her eyes closed and all kinds of wires and tubes attached.

"Look," I said to Janie. "See her pointed lips. I told you they're tough."

Janie giggled, and Laura opened her eyes and rolled her head to look at us.

"I brought you two presents, Laura. Here's Janie. Mission accomplished."

Janie smiled at Laura and said, "Get well. I don't know what I'd do without you."

Laura gave a slight nod and blinked her eyes at me.

"Oh, yes, present number two. Mission accomplished, so here's your cell phone back."

She gave a little 'no' shake of the head and spoke in a weak voice, barely audible. "You keep. You got my number." Then she closed her eyes and drifted off.

I drove Janie back to Chisholm, and she slept curled up on the bench seat of my truck, oblivious to the smell of Lucky's blood in the cab or my dried blood on the seat-back. Francine and Alex greeted us at the Clayton residence, having gotten word on the night's happenings. Mom and daughter hugged and cried and laughed, and Alex and I left them to talk it over with each other, as we went back to my bungalow.

I had a six-pack of green Rolling Rock bottles in the fridge and I popped the caps. We guzzled, and he said, "Damn, this is better than canned shit anytime."

"Sorry I don't have any Twinkies to go with it," I said.

"It's good, as is." He looked at the bottle. "What's this '33' on the bottle mean?"

"Nobody knows. Some say it means 1933. The year Prohibition was repealed. Others say it is the number of words in their brewing pledge."

Alex read the pledge on the bottle and then counted the words. "Sonofabitch. Thirty-three words, exactly."

I shrugged and swallowed some of mine. "Who knows?"

"I got some info you'll appreciate hearing," Alex said. "Got the word earlier they picked up Jerry Crawford. KBI got him out in Dodge. He was on his way to Colorado with a load of pipe bombs."

"Well, that's good news," I said, and then I told him about Buford Thomas.

"Hells-fire, Jimmy, I buy it. It doesn't surprise me one bit. I'll check it all out, but I agree with that friend of yours at WPD. This ain't gonna hold together, not even with chewing gum, not for no jury." He downed a half a bottle in one gulp and looked me in the eye. "I got a job waiting for you, Jimmy."

"What do you mean?"

"With Phil out, we're down a man and I gotta replace him. You're just what we need, so the job's yours."

"Alex, you know I gave all that up, after what happened to Sondra. I just want out of the life. I took on Vernon's case because it was family and friends."

"It'd be different up here, not like it was down in Wichita with WPD."

"Different? Like a murdered sister and Vernon Johnson and a Mexican drug ring? That kind of different?"

"You know what I mean."

I just stared at him.

He gulped the second half of his bottle, set it down hard and said, "You think about it, Jimmy. You think about it."

40

A few weeks later, my long awaited date with Charlie proved anything but disastrous. My meal was a hit by anyone's standards, but then I don't think that's what she was keeping account of. I don't kiss and tell, but when she left the next day, she did, without a doubt, have a smile on her face. Then again, so did I.

I don't think I've ever heard the term Lorna Doone issued forth as a long extended scream before, but the words are still echoing in my head.

After Laura had fully recovered from her gunshot wound, she and I made frequent trips to Francine and Janie's house where I cooked barbeque for them out on their cement patio, and Janie fed and watered her unnamed puppy, a ten-week old yellow Labrador Retriever that Francine got for her from a local breeder. It cost Francine two week's wages at her new job as a cashier at Bob Johnson's hardware store, a job I helped to secure for her.

But she was proud of what she'd given her daughter, and would not be denied the honor of paying for it.

I'd picked out a book of Seamus Heaney poems to give to Janie as a present. One poem in the volume, entitled "Weighing In," implies that all things come into balance eventually. I just don't know if it happens in this lifetime or not. Then again, the final line of the poem reads, "At this stage only foul play cleans the slate."

While I marinated chicken in my patented red sauce, Janie tossed a Frisbee to her Lab, who was too young to catch it and had no idea what the game was all about, not understanding the "retriever" part of his title yet. Laura chatted with Francine and LaVonda Johnson about gender issues. Bob, who was as he put it, pleased as punch to have Francine working for him, poured charcoal into a cast iron grill.

"She's just the hardest working little lady I ever had behind the counter," he said.

"I'm glad it's all worked out, Bob."

"I guess good things can come outta bad when all is said and done." He squirted lighter fluid in the charcoal and thought for a moment. "Do you think justice will be done?"

"I can never guess what the criminal justice system will do in any given case, but I do think Buford Thomas will pay for his deeds."

Buford had been arrested, and when confronted with the known facts, actually confessed to Vernon's murder. He seemed proud to admit to his accomplishment, and explain his intricate scheme of staging the accident after the fact, and acted as if what he'd done was the right and American thing to do. He even threatened the judge.

Janie walked over cradling the puppy in her arms. She wore a yellow and black WSU Shocker baseball tee-shirt Laura had given her.

"Mr. 'O,' do you think I'm crazy?" Janie squinted and looked intensely at me.

"Crazy?" I was turning chicken in the marinate, and I wasn't sure what she was talking about.

"Yeah. That guy who guarded me, Manuel, said I was just like the woman in the Yeats' poems I recited for him, 'Crazy Jane,' only I was crazy Janie is what he said."

"You recited Yeats to Manuel?" I shook my head in wonder. "Janie," I said. "You are anything but crazy. You are, without a doubt, one of the most normal people I know."

"Okay, if you say so. You know, as a sort of memorial, I think I'm going to name my dog after him."

"Manuel? You're naming your dog Manuel?"

"No, Yeats. I'm going to name him W.B."

"W.B. That's a fitting tribute. By the way, I brought you a present, Janie. It's over there on the picnic table."

She opened up the sack I'd laid there earlier and pulled out the volume of Seamus Heaney poems.

"I think it's time you graduated beyond Yeats to something a little more modern in poetry."

Things really did seem to be going much better for Janie and Francine, although when I went into the kitchen to get Janie a can of pop, there was a carton of Marlboros in the refrigerator. The subject of human frailties often occupies my thoughts, and I wonder sometimes if life isn't just a succession of comings and goings from our own individual faults.

The events of those weeks last June and July eventually sorted themselves out, for the most part. Buford Thomas is serving a life sentence for the murder of Vernon Johnson. The evidence itself never would have convicted him, but his own arrogance and prideful confession put him in the state prison at El Dorado.

Clare Miller worked her way through the judicial system until she wound up at the Topeka Women's Correctional Facility, a combination medium and high security prison.

After Clare's arrest, the local paper ran a series of stories on the case and there was wide public interest. She took on somewhat of a mythic status in the articles, and became something of a local legend. One article contained a photo that had been found at the house by investigators showing the two sisters, Clare and Lael at ages six and seven, smiling and with arms around each other, sitting on a giant tree limb which hung out over the river. They also found a shoebox she'd hidden after murdering her sister. When the attorney recovered the box and brought it to Clare, it still contained a stack of songs written by Lael, songs that Clare's green-eyed monster wanted to keep hidden from her family at the time. The pages were yellowed and brittle, but still intact.

Clare began a series of jailhouse recordings, using Lael's songs and giving her credit for writing the music and lyrics. Her first CD release was entitled "Well-Heeled in the Hoosegow," and its cover has a picture of a single shoe lying on its side. It has a broken spike for a heel. Somehow, I picture Clare singing in her cell wearing only one shoe, endlessly limping and turning in her dance of futility.

I try not to give too much thought to events of the past, and Sondra's whispered admonition in my dream about an abiding peace has certainly helped me to do a better job of that, but sometimes I'm still pulled in. I listened to Clare's CD the other afternoon and thought about what led her to where she wound up, and what drove Buford to his maniacal killing rage. I did this while weeding out the dead herbs and trimming the winter-hearty ones back, out on my terrace.

Tiresias wasn't any help with this, but he sat close by staring at me as if he could see, and he probably could in his own way. He had a look of amusement on his wrinkled face. I am certain it was with his help I came to the conclusions I had about my ancestral violence following me and being hardwired for it.

I may not be able to escape it. Maybe I will have to live with it, but at least I may be able to bring some measure of balance into the equation, as the Heaney poem I gave to Janie implies. Maybe I help to even things out, even if it is with a little foul play.

I thought about Alex's offer and what I would say when he came back at me, like I knew he eventually would. Maybe Tiresias could help me make up my mind about that, too.

When I stood up with brown and brittle Rosemary sprigs in my hand and looked out over the stubble of wheat field, a Blue Heron flapped its wings, heading away from the river, and was probably giving thought as to whether it was time to head south yet. Tiresias would soon burrow into his nest for hibernation, and I wouldn't see him again until spring.

Deep within, as I looked at the scene and took in its spare beauty, I truly did feel that the land itself contained some sort of an abiding peace, and that it always would.

*****

About the author: Conrad Jestmore has published short stories, poetry, plays and non-fiction in numerous journals and anthologies, and is a Past President of the Kansas Writers Association. This is his first novel. He has earned gainful employment as a welfare case worker in the mountains of northern California, an elevator operator when elevators still had them, a bartender, a paint warehouse stocker, a USO performer and a high school teacher. He is a Reiki Master and currently teaches Reiki classes and heals both humans and animals in his central Kansas Reiki practice.

*****

COMING IN NOVEMBER, 2012:

Fields of Death

Book 2 in the Jimmy O'Reilly mystery series

Made in the USA
Charleston, SC
25 September 2012